Terracotta Dreams

A Book of Poems and Musings

By

Monalisa Joshi

Become
Shakespeare
.com

First published in 2018 by

Becomeshakespeare.com
Wordit Content Design & Editing Services Pvt Ltd
Unit - 26, Building A-1, Nr Wadala RTO, Wadala (East),
Mumbai 400037, India
T:+91 8080226699

WORDIT ART FUND

This book has been funded by WORDIT ART FUND
WORDIT ART FUND helps deserving Authors publish their work.
To apply for funding, please visit us at
www.becomeshakespeare.com

ISBN:978-93-87649-03-3

Disclaimer

This is a work of fiction. Names, characters, business,
place, event and incidents are either the product of the
author's imagination or used in a fictitious manner. Any
resemblance to actual person, living or dead or actual event
is purely coincidental.

Dedication

This book is dedicated to my loving husband and my two adorable sons Aditya and Tanmay. It is for their constant love and support and my abiding passion for poetry that this book has come to life.

Contents

Acknowledgement

Breathing in a mundane world, my verses comes from those corners of life that could not be spoken in words otherwise, and had I not been blessed with this gift of writing my soul would have felt much clogged and wouldn't have forgiven me. Therefore feeding my soul's hunger I indulge in writing with all my passion and now it has become an uncanny reflection of me. Yet there are people who have been my constant support and my true inspiration. They have provided me with the vibes for creating this book and I wish to express my gratefulness towards them.

Firstly; a huge thanks to my God for bestowing me with this beautiful gift of writing. Secondly a loving thanks to my two beloved sons. It is their being around me all the time and inspiring me with their innocence and exuberance both that I feel being the most blessed person on earth. From their glance and gestures towards me, I can sense that they are the biggest admirer of me both as a mother and as a writer. Also huge thanks to my husband of course, since he is a mute supporter and observer and utters no word but I sense a big 'Yes' in his gestures towards my dreams. And also I want to thank my beautiful mother whom I have always looked up to and it is she who has taught me kindness, love, strength helping me in being and becoming the woman today I am.

Moreover I believe that love is the element that inspires me to write fantasy poems, romance and love poems, ballads and more. Maudlin emotions also inspire me to write but it is glee when I am most productive. So I am also thankful to all the human emotions that often stir inside me and helps me in penning them down into poems and more.

Lastly I am sincerely thankful to Mr.Uzair Thakur for recognizing my work and forwarding my Poetry manuscript to Wordit Art Fund. Thus to him and to the entire team of Become Shakespeare; I express my earnest gratitude for making my dream come true of becoming a published author and a poet.

Preface

'Terracotta Dreams' is a poetry book with eighty poems inked inside its chest. The book has myriad emotions that often stir inside the author's heart and have been narrated and given wings through verses, ballads, musings and more. Nonetheless; the poetess believes, dreams are defiant and this book therefore reveals myriad truths and shades of her prosaic life.

This book showcases the writer's belief that love and romance are two blissful elements on earth, but they also bring along their counterparts disguised as pain and hurt. Yet they have added to the author's luxury by enabling her to give much volume to the book as it depicts many soulful love poems and some morose poems reflecting the dread in the path of love as both goes hand in hand. This volume thus contains thousand words of dismay and maudlin confessions stringed into poetry.

An amalgamation of various moods and emotions, this book is a journey of the poetess into those hidden corners where often nostalgia wraps her into its opulence giving words to her yearnings. She seldom finds herself a hermit who is wedged amid the chaos of a mediocre life, desperately in search of solace and finds poetry as her escapade from all the plethora of drama. However; amid the mayhem and mixing emotions into art the author relishes in tagging herself as a romance writer as the book contains several fantasy and whimsical love poems that depicts the earthly love and the beauty of a man woman liaison.

'Terracotta Dreams' is truly an idiom to many of her heart's innermost feelings and her poetic musings. As often, walking on the path of mundane she feels that her dreams are fragile alike an earthen pot that appears harsh on the surface but the inner core is delicate and can be broken easy. Consequently, she wants to capture them all in verses before the dreams become kaput and decays in some dark corner. Furthermore, as an Indian woman she takes pride in her womanhood and feels that she has a deeper connection to the bygone era and it is the lineage that she feels obligated to carry over her shoulders and keep her tradition alive, which she has inherited from her maternal dwelling. Thus, dangling in the midst of love and hurt, tradition and her sense of belonging to a bygone era, this book showcases both contemporary and her traditional narrative style of writing that she has portrayed through mixed genre poems.

The book also brings forth myriad of her soulful musings that will linger long even after the book is finished reading. All the poems are written in an intrigue, captivating and in a story telling way as the book somewhere will take the reader into a world of alluring ballads with long poems and somewhere into the poetess's candour reminiscences. The tale in each poem becomes alive with great imagery, rhyming, free verses and her contemporary style of writing. Nevertheless the book itself is a journey of a woman and a poetess disguised behind the ebb and flow of human emotions.

A Poet's Confession

There was a door left ajar,
To a room where the light,
Was dim, and letters I saw,
Were dancing in chirping joy,
My heart beating swiftly now,
I went inside and saw on the chair,
Was sitting fiction and writing itself,
He held my hand and said,
Write, you write!
And I took the pen, as I was,
About to write some fiction,
Of characters myriad,
And stories untold,
His sister poetry got upset,
She dragged me by hand,
To another world of flying words,
Bathed my soul into ink,
That was as black, as shadow
Mine, but I had a new pen,
A golden pen, she grinned,
And said,
Write, you write!
And I took her pen,
Soon I began to write,
Verses myriad, weaving dreams,
Making love with lover mine,

Times as much I desired,
Romance sat on the same,
Couch I had once sat by,
Of maudlin emotions, poetry,
Gave me wings to soar,
She became my mate,
And I her soul mate!
Yet again in that room,
Her brother came, 'Prose'!
And said to me annoyed,
How naive of thy mind,
Write me, you write!
And gave me the silver pen,
I took it and wrote stories,
Few, and oft they stole,
My sweet slumber, they,
Haunted me in places all,
Where my heart feared,
To dwell, they were so real,
Oh! The characters were real,
That's how he made me write,
And soon I surrendered,
Oh! Yes I succumbed from prose,
And ran away, to meet fervor,
Mine, she was not in that,
Room anymore, left long ago,
Poor me couldn't I keep her,
Safe in my heart, she was like,
A soothing gust that came with,
A flow, and so I crossed,
The meadows of lore,
Swimming through the,

Rivulet of ballads, and climbing,
The mountains of sonnets,
At last found her in the shrine,
Of youth, waited she for me,
She never grew old, only me,
And I held her hand, she kissed,
On forehead mine, like a,
Mother to her child I took,
Refuge into her lap till eternity...

Ashes

There was an urn that stood clandestine,
Within a wooden closet, was never meant to,
Be taken nor touched, behind the wall of,
Few attires it was resting in silence and,
Darkness brooding much, only he knew!

And with every dew of dawn's cascading,
Influx and of virgin beam peeking through,
The casement of his dwelling, that came from,
The heaven's gate, sitting on the chariot of bate,
Asking evermore to give them the urn and,

Delay no further, but the ever adamant lover,
Of his muse laughed deviously, for he knew!
None could, not the humans on the land, nor,
The birds of the blue, and neither even the
Goblins disguised as men could ever steal,

That golden urn, that he had kept safe in a,
Situate where he only knew, but to his dismay,
The sprites heard his thoughts in his deep,
Slumber, when he was in dreams with his,
Beautiful wife, wandering as earthly lovers in,

The garden of love, naked as they were busy,
Making love, the sprites found the keys to,

The most clandestine closet, from his fallen,
Attires and stole the urn, making it vanish,
Forever, protecting it now in their safekeeping,

Another most clandestine place for him to,
Know, but with dawn he came to knew of,
This blasphemy, and cursed all the men, the,
Birds, the earth and the sky, the goblins and,
The gods they were all his culprit and he loathed,

And despised for stealing that urn, but he wasn't,
The one, a weak lover, a weak husband but an,
Insane man whose confines were broken, he tore,
The sky, he dug the chest of earth, he ripped,
Many souls to find the way to that golden urn,

His fright reached to the heavens and hell,
The golden gates were guarded with them,
Goblins, waiting for the lone lover to come,
To slay and tear his body in parts two, one falls,
On the land and one into the blues, where the,

Scavengers shall tear his soul apart, and he,
Would then wander, forever a soul, a scold,
For playing it with the gods, yet he came,
Crossing the rivers of blood, sin and more,
Slaying the goblins all, he stood in front of,

Him staring directly into his eyes, the voice,
Roared and asked, "Why have you come?"
He pointed towards her, who was standing,
Behind, gazing quietly with hope many in,

Eyes that twinkled like a star and tears incessant,

Like a rivulet, she stood with chained feet,
And hands, she was stuck here for that golden,
Urn, her ashes rested in it, and he wouldn't,
Let her go, keeping her soul in that urn safe,
And in heart his, but to see the chastisement,

His dead wife was in, alas! His eyes got wet,
And for the first time, in many years he knelt,
And cried like a child, how could he let her,
Go, the ashes were all he had of his bereaved,
Wife, they both cried and seeing their love,

The man in the golden robe shed tears few,
Giving back the golden urn, whispered in,
Ears, free the ashes, free thy wife, for it is,
Thy love that chains her here let her go,
Her role here is through; let her be born again,

And he fell on his divan, from his slumber,
He rose and found it was but all a dream,
The urn was never touched, it was there,
Her wife's ashes were resting within, only,
He knew of what pang his heart was in!

The aloofness that he was decreed with,
His rage was against them, he feared none,
And didn't let go of his beloved wife's ashes,
Prepared again to take the, wrath of the Gods
And goblin men, he couldn't but let his wife go...

Awakening of Nari

He mixed the clay from the,
Rivulet of heaven for days seven,
And sculpted a delicate statue,
With lustful eyes, his amorous,
Hands carved a figure that seemed,
Fragile with pair of bosoms,
Soft as the fresh season's plum,
And pink as cherry blossom,
He took ample clay and made tresses,
Long that shall flow as rivulet,
When the zephyr teases and pleases,
All those eyes of men,
Who shall see the statue of dust!

And when the forefathers asked why is,
He creating another human after man,
And what name shall he give to,
His artistry, he said, "a man's heart,
Is incomplete without its opposite,
Thus I have created a woman, who shall,
Bear both man and woman, she would,
Be the goddess of all on this earth,
But I have made her delicate,
She shall have no power over us,
It is we, us, man, who will slave her,

And so shall she be the goddess of beauty,
Of lust, and her youthful skin will fulfil,

Desires of a man till night, till dawn,
And she will remain an object with,
A beautiful body, fragile ah! My finest,
Creation a woman! Yes I shall call her,
This and she would bow to me,
With her head forever bowed unto my feet,"
Said the younger one in the heaven,
And gave life touching her heart,
Awakened she opened her eyes, there was,
Lightning and thunderstorm that,
Roared into the skies, her cheeks soft,
Red with rage now her fingers thin,
Lifted the spade to kill her lustful creator,

Hath thee lost thy mind?
Thee hath aroused a goddess's anger,
And see now what catastrophe to befall,
Her naked body you have touched,
And spared be shall not one of us,
Her feminine aura rises from her hymen,
She shall bear the fruit of humanity,
In her chastity and run thy race,
See man! Oh see! What have thee done?
Reverse thy artistry, reverse thy lust,
And create a woman only for love,
The younger one bowed in shame,

Trahimam! Trahimam! Trahimam!
My creation can't be undone,
And unable I am to quash this,
Forgive me my forefather said he,
Her corporeal body shall remain sensual,
Forever till eternity, but she shall be loved,
More by man and man would be her,
Twin flame on her bodily journey,
I am giving her all the strength to endure,
Down there in a world full of men now,
But soon she shall make more of her,
Kind and they all shall be the goddess,
Of hymen, and her energy shall flow,

Through all living beings,
And man shall know her as woman, Nari, Stri!
Tathasthu! Tathasthu! So be it, so be it!
Said all the gods and the beautiful woman,
Smiled covering her figurine,
With her long tresses! Her lotus hands,
Then blessed all the Gods!
Then blessed all the men!
And the Gods bellowed roaring the skies,
Shakti Swarupini, Namastasyai,
Namastasyai Namo Namaha!

Glossary

Trahimam Spare me
Nari Woman
Stri Woman

Tathasthu so be it
Shakti Power
Swarupini Taking a form
Namastasyai Namo Namaha Salutations to the goddess

Baring

The hours of darkness seemed long,
Sitting by the window in her hearth,
The gust whispered in her ears the silent,
Words of love, the stars twinkled in far,
Sky, yet couldn't stand the sparkle of her,
Tears, she was longing that unison again,
Her heart beating fast and loud for him,
Beneath her tender bosom, half covered,
Half revealed, her voluptuous figurine,
With thin muslin, flowing along breeze,
Oft! The Romeo gust touching her skin,
Gentle like feather, playing with tresses,
Long, lost in the dreams of her beloved,
Realized never the stars, the sky and gust,

All ogled her earthly beauty, desiring to,
Embrace, snuggle, stroke and unveil her,
Her velvet skin, her dusky tone, her baring!
And seize benefit of her lover's absence,
She seemed alone, alone and hollow for,
Long now, days and nights and seasons four,
Were passing fast, they all wanted the same,
But her rigid heart knows the game,
Kaput she seemed fragile with tears,
Myriad that always rested on the side,
Of her eyes, every night she became this,

Goddess of covetousness sitting on the facade,
Of huge window on the top, from where,
Flows her white muslin and flows her breaths,

Infinite, on which sits his name, she yearns,
Oh! She yearns for him desperate, keeping,
Safe her soul from them, who fetch souls at,
Midnight, dark hours is their chosen time,
They all sing along the same havoc rhyme,
They come in many and one, only for fun
Nature their best disguise and all they want,
To touch her, kiss her, lust her, rust her,
Dust her, choke her, tear her, and eat her,
And day one the wind the strongest flirts,
Blew away her veil revealing the concealed,
Truth, bud of chastity waiting to bloom,
Feeling guilty she stood, shivering in her coy,
And the gust, the sky and the stars whom,

She had befriended in her solitude,
Seemed dryads, hidden behind their godly,
Attires, lust spilling from their eyes,
The gust with its might scratched her, nabbed,
Her, grabbed her, pushed her, threw her,
The sky laughed and laughed watching,
In delight, the stars shining brightest upon,
Her fragile body, that had remained veiled,
In darkness for long, her coyness was strong,
They snatched her timidity and threw it on,
Earth, and the earth cried and cried on that,

Monalisa Joshi

Bloody site her shrieks reaching where,
Someone still loved her, thought her more oft!

Shared intimacy long time back, and tonight
On his bed, he felt her cold breaths and more,
He was restless, the strong built earth skinned,
Twisting and turning on the sheets white,
On which the two have stayed whole night,
Awake and alive once, breathing and moaning,
Kissing and embracing, sinking and melting,
Deep into each, the warmth of his nest,
The days and nights were all like fest,
Alone in his huge abode, which she left,
A small mayhem, a small turned big,
And long enough their hearts don't dig,
On dead past, yet the wall wasn't broken,
The creepers of emotions on both sides,

Rising on wall hidden like their love,
He rose, a strong shadow in dark, slipped,
Into his silken robe, he ran, he glided,
Towards her abode, the more the near,
And his heart feared, and his heart feared!
And his eyes wide to see! She was eaten,
She was beaten, she was fallen, woman!
So fragile, alas! He was too late,
The merchants of soul, the seller in nights,
Took away her's and he could only,
Watch, her beautiful body covered in red,

Seeing her lover in front of her,
She rose and ran, her skin still velvet,
Her body youthful, her face like sherbet,

Red and cold, she fell into his arms,
He held her tight, in his valour,
She stayed whole night, she stayed whole night!
She had been for long, in the dark times,
Awake, thinking of his essence, feeling it more,
Of love, that came short but gave glee,
Pouring her senses all with his masculinity,
What nights of romance, ah! What nights of love,
When he touched her soul deeper,
Her baring was all sense when, oh dear!
Into his embrace feeling safe, no fear,
Her heart is all his now, she has wrapped herself,
Like a cocoon, he protects,
With his strength, her timidity!

Beau's Elixir

Sitting in front of mirror, combing her tresses,
The restless mind lost in chaos of yore days,
A tear twinkled, finding its way down cheeks,
Ludicrous battle of words broke the ties easy!
Wounds in heart still ooze blood melancholic,
Her senses still richly filled with his essence,

Oh! She has smelled many and more elixirs,
Yes she has smelled of flowers, of perfumes fine,
Of fresh morning breeze to the prayers divine,
Of warm slumber afternoons, to the last dew dusk,
Of night's cold robe filled with twinkle mass,
But her senses filled only with his essence!

That musk aroma from his body, his clothes,
Lingering yet within her, her chastity, her soul,
On the bed, on the sheets where she sleeps alone,
The closet is left with no clue, of his belongings,
But still his essence, oh! That masculine odour,
And only her senses filled with beau's elixir...

Beneath the Sepulchre

I heard some noises myriad nights,
A woman snivelling, her voice,
Low audible to me, yet sensed,
I, the hollowness trapped in heart,
Her's, there was a tale of pang,
Some hidden bruises still hurting,
And in her mellow voice she sung,

I heard night after night, her sobs,
And songs of her maimed heart,
She sung the tales of her kaput,
Love, the darkness she was caught,
In, the smell of mud filling into her,
Lungs choking to death, her howls,
Were like a banshee, I had chills,

Down my vertebrae, yet there was,
A lot alike to her tale and mine,
That hypnotised my soul to her's,
At last! The wall broke on the day,
When I was put to rest on white satin,
The whole world left with some tears,
In my solace, I opened my eyes again,

And saw the reflection of my peaceful,
Face, the mirror beneath the sepulchre,
Unveiled the truth, that woman was me,
I had been caught for long inside that wall,
And what pity, Alas! I couldn't save me,
From mayhem, and chose to sing and cry,
So I closed my eyes and never opened them...

Bleeding Words

It was a white paper, oh! Her heart was a white paper,
She wrote with the ink of love, she wrote with the ink
of passion,
Every word on the white became gold, and so the story
begun,
Happiness, dismay and mixed emotions she wrote and
wrote,
The pages soon became book, filled only with love and
love,
Pulping desires melting like fire, she had woven the
book,
With golden thread of her feelings, oh! She felt so much,

With time, she felt perhaps much, she got merged,
Somewhere, nowhere, where the words had any
meaning,
The nights are sleepless; mindless her thoughts are
many,
Staring the blankness, keeps talking to herself in silent
words,
Going berserk perhaps or she feels too much, that curse
again,
She is shouting, slamming like insane, the doors to the
heart,
Are locked forever, now the book lies somewhere in
dust,

Entangled in the web of dying love, and paralytic emotions,

Ego, attitude, arrogance all are culprits they killed her lover,

She is looking for him, amidst and across the cells were the,

Criminal lives, who took him so far, far in the loveless land,

She is feeling the pain deep; the words are bleeding, dying slowly,

Her words are bleeding; no one can see the red,

The rain started long before she realized, washing away the words,

Alas! In the wetness of her heart's tear, she stands bare feet,

She needs that one hand of love, lost in the world of life,

Still scribbling on the washed away words, rewriting hard,

Trying to find what they meant earlier, oh! The pages are red,

She has now written her last words with little breaths left in her,

Slowly wrapping herself into that book, if someone ever reads,

If someone ever reads those bleeding words, holding truth much,

Shall know the story, love didn't die on its own, it was murdered!

Cage of Love

I was the prisoner of your love;
I was the prisoner of a rigid wall,
Caged long inside the space,
Shared we under one roof,
Time was fading away swiftly,
Stole myriad moments of glee,
I looked at my skin, it was tight,
I gazed my face on the mirror,
It spoke of my inside fight,
I had lost my glow, the light,
You cared less, and I dared less,
One day seemed like years passed,
In aloof I sat, and in silence I cried,
My tears hidden and lips never smiled,
I knew never what you felt!
But only abhorrence I smelt,
Once love, and once loathsome,
Concealed gestures of face handsome,
I realized hating you was hard,
More than loving and I looked at sky,
With hope in eyes, and before the,
Ocean of dismay, pulled me beneath,
I chose to live forever in the sheath,
Like a cocoon and someday I shall fly,
My truth is undeniable, not a jargon,
I am living in a cage, only now I have,

Filled it with love, your love chains me,
Your hatred drains me, a blind contract,
Perhaps made before even we were born,
But I am at peace now living alongside,
In the cage of love, a prisoner of life,
Of you as my beloved!
Of you as my soul mate!

Camaraderie of Twilight

The cascading crimson hues from the heavens,
Sulking into the cerise warmth, gazing her skin,
Turning gold, a droplet of sweat slipping by,
The forehead of dawn, she quivered in her coy,
Shell gazing as startled, his hushed murmurs,
Of taking control, offering his authority in most,
Sauvé way, the few remnants of dawn had fallen,
Hitherto still refuting to abscond, swiftly began,

Gathering from the leaves, from the Marigolds,
And shaking the boughs she climbed and stole,
The essence of fresh morning mist, that when fell,
On earth filled the air with alluring petrichor smell,
Timid dawn backing off and twilight scattering his,
Wings, over the mowed grass, their parting took,
Place, light becoming shadow beneath crimson tide,
The dominion was ominous, lovers of twain bereft
souls,

'Camaraderie of Twilight' wasn't celebratory evermore,
Vulnerable beloved his, was murdered every day and
she,
Died with compliance, the silent love of the dawn was,
Not adequate for twilight, he seeks the sulking charm
of,

Night, melting into her arms he expresses infidel love,
Solemnity towards the mistress, defying the comfort of,
Dawn, who waits on another horizon with tearful eyes,
Gazing in silence her beloved becoming indiscernible,

'Camaraderie of Twilight' she longs more than night,
The longing of her's remaining as an unquenched thirst...

Courtship

With dawn I followed the dew,
Drops on the green, they dripped,
In concert and the soil quenched,
Its thirst of desire, waited thy soul,
Night whole, alike the parched,
Earth, the dews from heaven,
Filled its lust and once barren,
Its coffer is filled with pride,

And in solace in that wrecked,
Dwelling, with one bed,
With dust much and less bread,
Thy breaths I hear rising high,
Your manhood roared, dared I,
Cutting loose all the decrees,
There was no contemplation,
For future, neither I looked back,

What was left in the past!
This time, I had waited long,
My footsteps were known,
Even before reached thy abode,
The moon was the only mate,
I had on my path to thy solace,
And twain hearts burning in fire,
For long, the beats even louder,

And desires rising spilled out,
I saw you standing on the facade,
Thy bare skin and I gazed akin,
Runneth came I into thine embrace,
There were no qualms, the night,
Grew long, glancing in quite,
Our covetous love, that happened,
Night after night!

Myriad words of despise,
Myriad ears of spies spreading,
News to corners and more,
Tagging incestuous our love,
But cared we never, it was love,
Desires and more, feeling no guilt,
Ever we oathed to be this forever,
Tis, our courtship needs no name...

Dark Mirrors of Haven

The raft was moving slowly, shoved by gentle waves,
Realizing it was a vast ocean, she was soon wide awake,
She was stuck amid, she cried for help million times,
Her eyes saw many shadows moving fast on the surface,
They came fast; her subtle body lying motionless,
The shadows prying all over her, she couldn't resist them,

The waves have brought far, her raft floating in the,
Black ocean carrying its dark brackish water along,
She made her way to a haven, passing through gazing eyes,
Amid many faces, the windows were covered with glasses,
There were many colours, yet strange dimness in the haven,
She saw the same water on the floors of that space,
Its walls were badly dampened, feet sinking till ankles,

She strolled in quiet, saw many women stood by,
The doors with chained feet, their faces painted,
Like clowns, there were no expressions on them,
It seemed eternity, age, time and feelings caged,
Behind the door, on which hung a gigantic lock,
She passed across that alien hall, knowing not,

Where she stood, and suddenly was dazed to see,
A woman imprisoned behind a mirror, and many,
She saw, they were shouting, banging their heads,
On those dark mirrors, trying hard to break free,
Alas! Those mirrors were hard like frozen ice,
She started trouncing on the mirror too, to help them,

Oh! She couldn't! Alas! She couldn't,
Break those dark glasses; her eyes now fell on,
That young girl who stood apart and alone,
Framed beneath another mirror dark alike,
That girl pointed her finger trying to presage,
To look behind, please look behind!
Someone slapped and the sound was loud,

The voice said! "How much need I pay?"
And she fell into her body, eyes still gazing the roof,
It was over, fast and quick,
"She makes no tantrums, she is good", the voice said,
Why would she? It was the den of iniquity,
And stuck was she like all else, floating in the same
dark ocean,
Perhaps the truth hidden inside their chest,
Was much painful and unseen …

Darling Look at Me

I have known you long, staying along,
Spent myriad moments of togetherness,

Yes! An invisible air been suffocating us,
Yes! Few intruders have been invading us,

Do not forget, Ah! My beloved, my soul mate,
It was our nest, with weeds of love we made,

I smell irk, I sense restless twain hearts,
Still beating for each other, let the serpent,

Know; kill its heart with dagger of love,
Alas! It took you along and far you stand,

Visible to my eyes, I see you from behind,
Your manly figurine is still so desirable,

I was deep hurt in moments your never,
Looked behind, I was there, like a river,

Flowing with waves of melancholia,
The ebb and flow of dismay, waiting to touch,

Thy body, and submerge you along into me,
Hear please my silent sighs of despair, hear me!

My soul kept shouting amid mundane tides,
Darling look at me for once, I am still crying,

Waiting for you to hear my silence, and my tears,
Waiting for you forever, trapped in thy love dear...

Derelict

Smell of antiquated breeze flowing within,
The place was lulled and stood hollow,
The fractured walls, broken window panes,
A dead house long ago perhaps, holding,
Myriad stories of glory and romance,
Sunk in its heart deep within, waiting!

To be told, often passing by I gazed at,
The ruined wretched house, speaking to me,
In endless words like a child, audible,
To me, once I dared crossed the fences,
And entered within a void space with,
A torn sofa filled with dust, nothing much,

Some broken and corroded utensils,
Lying in the kitchen, all dust upon,
And webs all, some broken pieces of glass
Bangles, a faded photo of a woman,
Lying on the floor, few old newspapers
That fled with the breeze and amid,

These I saw the glee, I felt the time,
Of a tale left behind, those joyful faces,
A handsome man and a beautiful woman,
Sitting on that sofa holding each other,

Like a bioscope images became alive,
Feeling the love of that love filled time,

My heart grew warm and the next,
Moment, melancholic, feelings stirred,
Tears found their way through eyes mine,
I knew nothing, nor the story, the people,
Yet there was something in the air,
That whispered in my ears the untold,

Tale of love, resentment and rejoice,
Perhaps it wasn't the skeleton house,
That stood still, it was the abyss of my own,
Heart, where I found my past, those broken,
Pieces of emotions, those empty spaces which,
Shall never fill, which might never fill!

It wasn't the derelict house, it was my,
Derelict heart, that still oozes blood,
I stood by the window, gazing quietly,
The gust came bringing all lost in time,
Stealing some solitude from the house,
One glance at the place leaving, I never turned behind!

Dilemma

The mirror is a liar,
Your eyes are too,
My face doesn't reflect,
In both anymore,
The music has been mute,
Your voice along,
Not anymore I hear,
The love filled care,
My breaths are impatient,
Your essence is there,
But not the warmth of,
Your breaths on my face,
I feel anymore,
Your presence is around,
But your embrace is gone,
Living or dying with this,
The Heart is sore,
A long departing it seems,
This time, for reason,
That faded long back,
Clinging twain souls yet,
In a string of mayhem,
Alas! What poignant dilemma...

Eccentric Aficionada

Saffron turban on the head,
Walking carefree upon sand,
The crimples and creases on his,
Clothe, bringing the scent of desert,
Bringing the scent of camel along,
A deal with the sun, fair one,

It promised, it would throw heat,
When his foot touches the grounds,
Of sand as far as eyes go, in the midst,
Of this heat, her lover comes from,
The farthest lands she has never seen,
He says it's there, and she believes,

Peering from the little window,
Of her mud home, certainly not big,
But a heaven inside, a bed with sheets,
Of dyed colourful cotton, with beads,
And mirrors, floor of straw and dung,
He comes inside, with half body bent,

Tall is lover hers', doors are small,
Masculine and tanned, all eyes,
Envy, women and men ardent,
To know amorous love saga of them

Hot days ties them in oneness,
Twain bodies wet inside the hut,

Nights are cool for him to return,
To the lands distant where he disappears,
With dawn, her eyes lay upon again,
On the dusty paths, where his footprints,
Remains; and walks on them with dawn,
Myriad feet, erasing her beloved's marks,

The moon and night silently whispers,
In his ears, to make him stop,
Forever, she desires the same, Alas!
The merchant of love is he, he sells love,
His caravan stops never, his camel rests never,
He is the eccentric aficionada,
Whom she has fallen in love with...

Escaping Words

Yes! I know he won't buy those roses,
Wrapped fancy fully in pink paper,
Tied with silken ribbons gorgeous with,
Their pretty curls, as we strode along,
The footpath and the vendor gazed on,

I knew he wouldn't let me stand and,
Gape those pretty blossoms, with a,
Hidden wish blossoming in heart mine,
Soon then I would run to catch up with,
His swift pace, taking one glimpse of his,

Silent face and mute eyes, I would know,
It then, he finds all this baloney and naive,
Oh! For god's sake be mature my wife,
There are myriad things to do, then buying,
Those flowers for you, which won't last a night!

Yes! I know there are myriad things to do,
And loving me was not one of course,
That night too, I remained again an observer,
Of his harsh expression, wondering evermore,
Where did that smile vanished, does it exists?

And again many more time and many times,
I fooled my soul, wandering and smelling,

Terracotta Dreams

In thin air the fragrance of romance bygone,
I knew it, yet hoped whenever came memories,
The days passed in silence and the dawns',

Cascading arrival on the doors of my heart,
With thuds of hope, I waited his arrival,
And the old spark to be ignited again,
Oh my! How naive of me to hope even,
My soul too forgot, flowing in the days',

Chore, I mistakenly made a castle of dreams,
Alas! His excuse's castle have become much,
Bigger than mine, his escaping words were
Resting evermore on his lips with an uncanny,
Silence that I could not bear and even tear,

Much has been mute, even the tick-tock,
Of the wall clock sounds loud now,
And yes I have to disclose, the couch,
Is my mate now, where I sit all by myself!
Writing poetry with a pen and a paper,

Did I tell you that black is my loved,
Hue now, at least it takes away the,
Black clogged in my heart, onto the whites,
I have learnt too scribbling few escaping words!
Which saves my from the plethora of,
That uncanny silence which I had,
Evermore mistaken as his unspoken love...

Fall's Unsaid Love

She stood in her coyness, covered in dew,
Her skin wrinkled and curled up not new,
The impish and naive gust of fall teasing,
Her overtime, the blossom of her youth,
Lost with myriad falls, perhaps it was last,
With one string her life attached, aghast!

She wanted back all in her lap, lost love,
Lost times of warmth and placate,
Seasons and fall her mates, standing oft,
In her galleria, she thought of grabbing,
All those moments of togetherness in fist,
Alas! Too small to catch the tick of mist,

Blurred vision had seen much, aloofness,
For them she is a wrinkled, saffron leave,
Ready to fall, love stuck clinging last heave!
Been long the parting had made sore,
At her last, recalling his last words for,
This fall remaining as his unsaid, said love,

Do not die ever, for I had loved you once!
Do not die ever, for I had loved you once...

Find Me, My Lover!

If you don't find me at home, do not bother,
Look for me in the broken pieces of your heart,
Look for me in the stolen moments of time,
Look for me through the past lanes of love,
Look for me where I have spent my childhood,
Look for me where I have stayed in my youth,

If you don't find me in your heart, do not panic,
Look for me in the places once we made love,
Look for me in the places we fought in havoc,
Look for me in those times when we grew old,
Look for me in those times when I left you untold,
Look for me if you haven't erased me from you,

If you don't find me in your breaths, do not agonize,
Look for me in the rhythms of your own breath,
Look for me in the abyss of your own hearth,
Look for me in the remnants of those moaning,
Look for me in the breeze that still flows in morning,
Look for me in the dusk's gust that still touches your skin,

If you don't find me in your soul, do not be miserable,
Look for me in the wrecked pieces of your body,
Look for me in the reflection of yours in the mirror,
Look for me in the wrinkles of your skin,

Look for me in the in the twirls of your veins,
Look for me in the damp corners of your eyes,

If you don't find me anywhere, do not be disheartened,
Look for me in the brooding darkness of thy abode,
Look for me in the silence of myriad fallen tears,
Look for me in the wait so long for you day and nights,
Look for me in the bait of past love, till dawn till dusk,
Look for me in the moments when we were together,

And still if I am not found, perhaps I had never existed,
And if I am found ever again, then I was always there...

Forever Lost

Oh! My beloved do not bereave me,
For I would not find the way home,
The paths are dark and alley so wet,
What if I slip and tumble away far,

I would be a lost cloud then, with gust,
Flirting and throwing me to places,
Never have I seen, do not turn away,
And abandon my fragile heart, what if I,

Am blown far off, with swag of wind,
I will be lost forever then, who shall?
Hold my hand and take me home,
Who will find me amid the crowd like own?

In the mirror of my heart reside thine,
Image, and the stories of our making love,
Inked in my nerves and blood,
The warmth of thine embrace still lingers,

On my soul and on my uncovered body,
And essence thine on my skin,
I keep gazing with fear, when left,
All by myself in the vast horde,

Of faces unknown as they watch in awe,
My perspiring face pale as bloodless,
But only my eyes keep searching for,
Thy sight, what if you forgot that,

Someone waited for you still there,
In the vestibule, and then I would be,
Lost, and taken away so far, tis, my fear,
Of being lost forever makes me cling more,

Want you more, even love you more,
Tis, deep fear, thy senses would ever know,
And I would be gone and lost forever,
Someday, before you would think of losing me!

Her Enemy! Her Lover

She was walking slowly under the stars,
Forcing her body against the storm,
The night was dark; she was wet and cold,
Following in the shadow of her lover's hold,
A strong built with a callous heart,
He thrashed her more oft, and laughed,
In his solace, she hated him yet loved,
Him ever more, but never read him more,
He was like an imp, with his deeds of despair,
Alas! That night when she was real hurt,
A thorn pricked in her heart deeper,
She bled and bled lying upon earth,
Her blood was much red than her lips,
Her pain visible on her face, she turned,
Slowly blue, frost taking over her skin,
She was to meet her end, one last time,
The eyes searched for him, her enemy, her lover!
And uttered his name for last in an insipid,
Voice, her cold breaths entering ears his,
He came running defeating the time,
Held his lady love whom he had hated,
All these years, his hatred was love of a kind,
He cursed her every minute, yet needed her,
He never gazed her beauty, yet knew she was!
And this time he pricked his heart against,
Her bosom, and let the thorn prick his,

He took it with a smile, and she was relieved,
The thorn went deeper into him, he still,
Smiled, and for the first time he kissed her,
Lips and for long, gazing her beautiful pale face,
Cupped in his hands, one last time he pushed,
Her out of the thorn and took it all on his chest,
He smiled in pain, and she watched in tears,
Her drops of dismay, her drops of pure love,
Fell on his cheeks and he closed his eyes,
There were no words greater than his odious,
Love, myriad left unspoken, yet he showed her,
He loved her; he had always loved her,
He now rests peacefully on her lap,
The storm was over, his breaths were too,
She never left, sitting there forever holding the,
Lifeless body of her sweet enemy, of her lover!

I Am Not a Goddess

Withered and tattered pieces fell,
From my bare body, emotions melting,
Down my cheeks, in white rivulet,
My eyes swollen red, I hide my face,
I stay behind the doors, a tiny space,
The curtains flow at times when soft,
Gust blows; it soothes me with the scent,
Of outside world, the parched land,
And wet drops on it, petrichor fills,
My soul and the fall's breeze comes,
Inside holding my hand it brings me,
Out of that void, I spread my wings,
Willing to fly, yet there are just sounds,
Of fluttering and I am deprived,
Knowing that my wings have been cut,
Haven't you been uncouth lately?
Forgetting oft that I am not a thing!

Alas! I'm lost much perhaps, in dreaming,
Days by, I am sitting there a lonesome,
And invisible body, why the past is such,
Stubborn, it takes me along into a land,
Where I was once turned to ashes, those,
Gloomy times when I felt wedged amidst,
Heaven and hell, yet my soul survived and,
Burning, it held my hand and conjured me,

From my own grave, I am living on this,
New facade now, where I have no friends,
Enemies none, my earthen dreams have,
Cracked, yet the cracks are not sign anymore,
Of my bleeding heart, I need no wings,
Yes! I am a wingless woman, I have the curves

Yes! They made me that way with a naive heart,
Why can't you see! I have come solely for you,
For love yours and romance, yet you kept,
Your face turned aside, I followed you and,
Fell, ah! What a spell, a sadistic cobweb,
That caught my soul this time, dead for,
Many nights laying a corpse in my own,
Dwelling, wasn't this the end! I am battling,
A mêlée day and night, inside of me there,
Are both paradise and abyss and you said!
Go to pilgrimage! Bow my head to whom?
My peace is devoured by you, my darling!
Making love to me still in times of havoc,
Haven't you been much demanding lately?
Forgetting evermore, that I am not a Goddess...

I Stood a Mannequin

He was babbling oh! In his slumber,
I heard from beyond, his words of,
Anguish, he thought he won the war,
Rules were his, laid upon me far,
Forgetting easy none escaped here,
None escaped the decay, his blood,
Running hot of youthful days, was,
With time now turning grey, freeze,
Taking control and much of paleness,
On his wrinkled face, yet he denied,
Of having ever been that callous,
He made a nest and there I rested,
For longer than I bear in mind,
Time really ditched me and ever,
I wondered what would halt this pain!
Would that man ever stops of loving?
Me desperate, his silence echoing,
Into my ears even here now, how can,
I be at peace beneath my grave,
When he walks with tears in his eyes,
And dropping few drops over the soil,
Where the last of me was buried!
I keep staring at heaven, pleading,
To them, how could I ask for his life?
That was not my dare, but seeing him,
Dying evermore pricked my heart with,

Thorns of our love, lost in space and time,
I paid my homage night and days,
To see he was taken care off, leaving him,
In the hands of those once we created,
With our bodily love, and I was at peace,
To see my values not gone wrong, he,
Kept his promise given long back then,
When he was just seven!
When he was just seven!
"When you go to heaven, Maa,
I will make a mannequin,
Of yours and give it to thy beloved and,
Keeper ours, that he never feels alone,
For then his eyes would be as blind,
And he would think of that lifeless doll,
As you and bellow, love, kiss, embrace,
Like he did then, when you were alive,
He would do it all, knowing not we made,
You a doll, yes we made you alike a doll!"
Making fool of him again and again,
Alas! Now when those days have begun,
I watched from the heaven, the man,
Cried more for me, I never uttered a word,
Neither I fought nor laughed on his absurd,
Jokes, he and I was alone in the darkest,
Room of life, I stood as a mannequin,
And he was alive breathing barely,
Oh! I cried more than him, wishing him,
Death more than life, old age was not,
He deserved, solitude shouldn't be his mate...

Indian Goddesses of the Kitchen

That place is their second home, where,
Most hours of their lives are spent,
Yes! There is a small temple which,
Isn't visited by the horde, but the Goddesses,
Live there, its' most often filled with smoke,
The overpowering smells of spices and herbs,
That stays on their hands, even when they,
Are done with their making varied victuals,
But how much their lovers crook their faces,
And nose while being passionate towards their,
Lady love, alas! That stubborn culprit stays long,
Those smell of garlic and pungent herbs remaining,
Still fresh on their hands and ordinary clothes,
Often becomes the reason for spoiling romance,
And again with dawn, the Goddesses awake,
Entering into their temple, awakening the steel,
Utensils with clamming sounds and when she,
Begins making the paste of spice over the,
Brawny chest of the grindstone, and her delicate,
Hands rolls the spherical stone crushing few chillies,
And cloves, it seems she crushes all her emotions,
Of her melancholic heart, and gets the paste,
Of love, for the grindstone's love for his Goddess,
Comes out as she smiles in solace collecting the,

Spice from its rock body, its chest then swells in pride,
For it remains the clandestine lover of hers',
Soon then the smell of the oil burning in the pan,
Fills into the nostrils of the inmates, as they,
Hide their sleepy faces beneath the pillows,
And silently cursing the Goddess for the chaos,
In that small, hot and murky place called the 'kitchen',
And then the whupishhh sound, the tempering,
Of bay and curry leaves, mixed with Asafoetida,
Tells her benign presence, into that smoky temple,
Where seasons' effects are the most,
Summer makes them prettier, with drops of sweat,
Sitting gracefully like pearls of salt on their forehead,
Which she carefully wipes now and then,
With one end of her sari, that stays tucked to her waist,
A serpent like braid also moves along with her,
Elegant pelvic moves, but she is not the one,
There to seduce thy lust, oh! She is busy to create,
Those divine delicacies to make their appetites roar,
Hoping to make way into the hearts of their men,
How naive! She is doing it day every, nights all,
Still trying to find the way to rule thy hearts,
But a twisted, discontented face she gets all in the end,
Even if there is a pinch of salt less or more,
If the red chilli has made the colour more crimson,
The Goddesses then have to listen to the,
Incessant complains and yet she manages to smile,
In the mid of that mayhem, knowing that another day is,
Going to be a struggle, to make that 'Perfect' platter,
That will erase all the downbeat thoughts from,
Their lover's mind, poor thing! Even the slumber,
Of these Goddesses are filled with the nightmares,

Of hollow boxes of supplies, and that challenging,
Question which evermore sits on their heads,
Like the 'Asura' whom once Goddess Durga,
Annihilated, but now he has taken disguise in the,
Form of that abiding question, what to make,
Today, tomorrow and day after tomorrow,
These Goddesses yet, in the mid of the chaos,
Often think while cooking, oh! That wedding,
Function is near; a birthday ceremony is approaching,
Oh my God! What will I wear, and in between,
Her vegan pot kept on low flame, she inquests into,
Her wardrobe, flipping and turning few saris,
Now the Indian Goddesses have the most critical,
Thing in her mind, during her respite from the kitchen,
She has to look beautiful, and when the day comes,
Her hands which had ruined myriad nights,
Of love making and seldom that romantic mood,
Of their lovers, but tonight she paints them in colour,
She wears her much worn silk Sari, even the jasmines,
Take pride in days those when she adorn them on her,
Neat chignon, yes! She knows when to be the queen,
Yes! She looks beautiful, the Goddess then roams,
Amid many of her kind, they all might be the slaves,
In their kitchen, but when outside they are the perfect,
Mistress of their men, albeit reaching home she shall again,
Jig into those ordinary crumpled clothes, no matter,
How messed up she stays, her dwelling remains neat,
She changes the sheet, but again her story from next,
Day begins into that kitchen, where turmeric will,
Ruin her beautiful painted nails, some will even crack,
But she won't bother; she finds solace in her little,

Kitchenette, and how much she does it fine, the belly of,
Their men would tell, yes! She will always be that,
Gorgeous mistress outside, without letting the world,
Know, her demeanour will be like an elite woman,
Who does no chores and has servants around,
The Indian wives know it all, they are the Goddesses,
Of the kitchen, undeniably the best aromas rise from,
Their kitchens when they are fully awakened,
As much they are the figurine of covetousness into the,
Eyes of their men, yes such Indian Goddesses do exist...

Glossary

Asura A member of a class of divine beings in the
Vedic period, which in Indian mythology tend to be
evil
Durga Hindu Goddess

Ivana

Oh! The petite damsel peeking from,
The mirror chamber, gazing quietly,
Never uttered a word to express its,
Existence but ah! What aroma, her fine,
Voluptuous figurine emitted, made him,
Drool nearer to her and he brought her,
Home, where his woman was waiting,
For his man to come and make love,

Alas! She smelt on his chemise perfume,
Fine, his cheeks blushing like cherries,
His face beaming with radiance she hadn't,
Seen in years, his lady love now spiteful,
Came closer and tore his chemise into,
Pieces many, threw him on the bed,
Bewildered much he behaved obedient,
She seemed like a tigress hunting her prey,
The man was in awe towards his fear-provoking,

Spouse and gone the session of earthly love,
Alas! Couldn't please his woman, her hawk eyes,
On him and her sniffing of his fair skin,
Made his pride fall in shame,
He stood as culprit, infidelity she smelt,
From his moustache and beard,
And a tear rolled down her cheeks,

The fear that she had lived for years,
And in her dreams, was coming true,

Quivering she took his coarse hands to,
Her heart that thumped loud and swift,
Beneath her supple bosoms, his heart now,
Dancing to the tune of her swift beats,
And their breaths uneasy to smell the chaos,
Coming and before he could utter true words,
She turned to him, there was a hard thud that,
Came to his twain ears, and his right cheek,
All turned pink from cherries red peek,

You cheat, you scoundrel am I not a,
Woman enough to make your desires,
Dance, am I not a woman enough to make,
Your life romance, spell her name or else,
Die in shame, and rot in hell forever,
For no man I could stand in here,
Carrying another woman's essence on his,
Chemise, and so I curse you to be eaten by,
Her and be never saved from that iniquity,

Ah! Poor lad, smitten all by his beautiful,
Lady love, said in a mellow voice, "her name,
Is Ivana, she rules my heart and senses five,
She is petite, voluptuous and a damsel in hive,
Ours, now ti's time oh! My beloved I chose her,
Over you and better you give thy consent,
For my love is pure for both of you,"
And soon he brought the glass bottle out,
Of his trousers and unwrapping the paper,

Covering from above the perfume's body,
Put it on his beloved's palm said in the,
Most alluring charm, "this my love is Ivana,
Another woman of glass bottle holding,
Fragrance of love inside her belly, ti's my
Lady is the other woman, will you let her,
Live into our nest, and on this blessed day,
I give it to you, shall you not keep good care,
Of Ivana" alas! Not bemused much she,

Took Ivana, threw it from the casement,
High of their fourth storey dwelling,
Aghast! His gusto turned in sheer dismay...

Jasmine Nights

A strange tune my heart is playing,
Today seems much known to me!
Romeo breeze has been playing,
All day long with my tresses and my skin,
I love sitting in my balcony,
Staring long the view outside,
The moment of emptiness,
The moment of be,
And that fragrance still lingers,
Of thy love, thy romance,
I feel nostalgic, with melancholic heart,
Today seems much known to me!
My tresses are loose,
Waiting for you to bring,
Those white flowers that,
I love to beautify on my bun,
When the whole night,
The sheets on the bed,
And even the bodies are filled,
With the richness of those white,
Flowers, and even when they die,
Keep spreading their fragrances,
So that our love lives, ever fresh,
Ever fragrant, like the dew drops,
The vendor sprayed, the whole night
Long, to keep his Jasmines' fresh,

He sold them, or did he sell love?
He knew never his few strands of flowers,
Brought us closer, much closer,
Tying us together like those Jasmine,
Tied to its string, never separated,
Even when they died, ah! What bonding,
My beloved knows I love Jasmine,
He buys me always and lovingly,
I tie them on my coiffure, I look beautiful,
And ask him the same question,
With silent gestures of mine,
There is never a word, but I can see,
In his eyes, his love for me!
I mutely thank him and always do,
The Jasmine nights, nights when the,
White buds of love had stayed with me,
Today seems much known to me...

Joven Sahib and Madame's Impious Love

Night of mayhem once witnessed bloody riots and
massacre,
The Joven Sahib went with his men, to defeat the army,
Of his enemies, there were many women, they heard,
Their hearts filled with excitement, bodies sweating
hard,
The Sahib and his men, went to avenge the murders,
Of their wives and people they loved, eyes red with
rage,

The fort that night saw a bloody sight, blood flowing
barbarously,
All men, women were killed, except one, she was
hiding,
Behind the curtains, she was a Royal English beauty,
Her white body was epitome of youth, weighing her
down with fear,
She looked like a fairy to those men, on earth that night,
The Joven Sahib made the hint, she was his catch,
The men left the room in silence, head bowed down,

It was always easy; eating the prey and filling the
tongue,
With their blood, but what jammed his feet tonight,

He felt sympathetic rather than anger, towards that
youthful body,
The Sahib took her hands and threw her in his jeep,
She made myriad shrills heard by unheard ears,
He took her inside his imperial abode in Nawabganj,

Dragging her into his room, adorned with dead skins
of animals,
The door was bolted; the house was filled with shrieks,
She was his prisoner and there was no escape,
The Royal Madame, with her refusing gestures first,
Ah! Fell in love, with the Sahib, he was fine looking,
Oh! She couldn't resist herself for the night to come,
To be alongside him and feel his body against her,

He saw approval in her moves, and fell in love too,
From the dark room of her life, there was a new dawn,
She was let out in the manor house, though watched
with,
Hateful eyes, their love was impious in that oriental
world,
She was not bothered but, for he loved her with passion,
They mated for life; she became his wedded companion,

And created history, the Joven Sahib and his muse,
Oh! What gracious sight of their love lock,
The night of massacre, created a story so wishful,
The bloody night, and many nights of lustful assault,
Culminated into love so pious, now they walked,

On the streets of Nawabganj, with nobility and dignity,
She was ever dead for her people, but here she lived,
And lived forever as Joven Sahib's Royal Madame…

Glossary

Nawabganj A small town by the Ganges in Kolkata

Kolkata Mindfulness

Resting like a cocoon it has been long,
I didn't realize when I became a butterfly,
Of human soul and had wings to fly high,
I was living there in her lap naively,
With eyes closed hearing to the town's
Lullabies that came from the hustle-bustle,
Of Nawabganj and of many things I didn't
Realize I had in my frock's pocket, as I roamed,
Around a little girl, but my soul an observer,
Oft brings back the reminiscences of those lanes,

I have walked, watching the ducks in the,
Green ponds, swimming and quacking,
Idly seldom times, on the still waters that,
Twinkled with the sunlight, they loved the sun,
Even on warm dawns, that started with the,
Smell of smoke rising from the dung and coal,
Stoves, the mud tilled homes and roofs,
And women wearing thick cotton saris,
Blowing the first fire to the mornings' sleep,
To be broken as the inmates too awake,

The mornings were always busy, not like here,
The women yelled, men shouted each other,
Amid their morning chores, those particular cries,
I had always enjoyed, they reflected love,

Warmth and care, I have seen yet not seen,
They were just scenes of a day in my life,
That I spent in there in holidays, now they,
Have become part of me, as I am far from,
Those smell of fish curries, cooked on earthen stoves,
Filled in the house of my uncle's and aunt's
The fish fresh from the Ganges, dipped fry,

What days were those! When careless and free,
I haven't thought would become part of me,
When I grow up, pushed far into the mediocre,
Life, yet I remember those slumbering noons,
When there were feasts in all the homes,
Of that narrow brick lane, the windows nets,
And slow moving table fans blew the essence,
Of delicious meat rice in the air, days on,
When our hunger roared with increased appetite,
Now no more are such feasts, nor those essences,

I smell, it wasn't only those days I miss, that love,
Of all the aunt's and grandma, fresh in my soul,
Fresh in my heart, the days are lying alive, when,
Small and curious I used to go to my grandmother's
Small room, where she sat and prayed for long,
Those many racks in her room filled with,
Idols and gods, she bathed those with sandal,
Paste and Ganges water, her white sari, the,
Sandal paste on her forehead, the Rudraksh
Necklace around her neck, that smell of her,

Being is still fresh in me; many are lost in time,
Or perhaps it's me, who has come lot ahead in time!

Those giggles and laughter of my childhood,
Audible only to me, when we pulled buckets filled,
With cool waters from the well, pouring over,
Each other and then shivered for long,
The mornings were fun even more when,
Children all made a gang to bathe in the Ganges,
For hours and hours the boys played, as I sat,
On the stairs watching the world moving slow,

The women cooked and gossiped, cared not I,
I had chirped and hopped from house to house,
Playing, and roamed around with my cousins,
On the evenings watching the sunset over the Ganges,
That crimson hue, the twinkling waves and the,
Sounds of the steamer still echoes inside of me,
The fresh cool breeze that touched our naive skins,
And our feet dipped in the pious river,
Time seemed frozen when, and the world small,
In here I feel seldom stuck, trying to go back there,

When I have seen those days of autumn,
Women dressed in white and red sari, playing
Vermillion Holi, as the air turned red, I saw,
Goddess in all, such beautiful red faces of joy,
I am far away now to all that's has been once,
My pride, now a hilly bride I am in another space,
I still pick pieces of broken earthen pots and smell
them,
Trying to feel the same essence, my childhood is caged,
In them, when we ate yoghurt from small mud pots,
I kept licking long even when the curd was done,

That taste of mud, I am so lost to find it back,
When the crowd of local trains agitated me,
But the ride on the ferry over the heart of the Ganges,
Overjoyed me, and one more time I want to live,
Again those childhood days spent in Kolkata,
To glimpse again those Raj structures, imperial,
But dead, I am still wandering in those streets,
Near the Fairy House, awestruck eyes I had always,
Dreamt of going inside, now only I have few grains,
Of sand stuck in my palm of past, of lost time,

And I don't know from where the tears come from,
When I wave that little girl, who waves at me,
With a big smile, resting as she sits beside her,
Beautiful young mother, the ferry keeps moving,
Farther and further, and I stand a mute observer,
Often nostalgic, I want to borrow some more glee,
From that girl's lap, and keep safe in my abode,
And the fragrance of tuber roses and jasmine from,
Nuptial nights I attended there, are fresh and reminds,
Me of lost, but not forgotten my Kolkata mindfulness...

Letter to the Beloved

Dear Beloved,
I shall keep the tea,
With smoke rising,
Resting on the table,
By the side of that bed,
Where for years,
We have been together,
I shall not remove the,
Curtains from the casement,
Not to disturb your sleep,
I shall not wash the linen,
And fill the space,
With the clatter of my chores,
And I will tell the world,
To come later for my sweet,
Beloved is at sleep,
I shall not make the steel,
Utensils crash on earth,
But I will cook some food,
And keep it warm in those pots,
On which we have together,
Shared numerous meals,
For last you would have my,
Hand cooked food, eat it with,
A smile and do remember me,
But do not cry, for the morsel,

Might cause some trouble,
Oh! My beloved, my soul mate,
I have to go now, I can't be late,
The chariot on which my soul,
Will depart has arrived on the,
Door and before the knocks,
Awake you, I am leaving you,
This day and it is going to,
Be as long as eternity,
Clad in that pink chiffon,
My attire is flowing with the,
Zephyr and I can't tell you,
How much I am missing you,
Already, the pain is more to bear,
My heart seems ripped apart,
But fate won this time,
I know if this day I leave, I shall,
Not be able to talk to you, for long,
I know silence will prevail in our,
Little dwelling, and you would,
Be running away from it,
But don't forget my darling,
In that silence I have spent years,
Waiting each day and night,
For you to come, standing on the,
Threshold with a warm smile,
But I must tell you that once,
I am there I shall wait for you,
Again just like I did on earth,
In that nest of ours,
And the day when you,
Will come, and if you are lost,

Do not be disheartened, do not,
Loose hope, just follow the smoke,
Coming from the roof of a small,
House and when you see neat,
Clothes drying on the clothes line,
And the floral essence of those,
Fills into your nostrils, do know,
Then, you have come home,
Because I shall always be,
There waiting for you,
I promise you will never miss,
The home you have left behind,
I will offer you the same love,
And warmth of my embrace,
Oh! My dear lover, for now,
I am leaving on the table,
My last words, a letter to you,
But by the time you read,
This I shall be long gone, but I,
Will always be inside your heart,
And read as many times,
For this letter would be my last,
Remnant belonging solely to you...

Yours,
Lady Love

Lineage

Yes! The mirror holds all the truth,
And that place where my reflection,
Falls, where I see the faces of those,
Women whom I have looked up to,
And dwelled in their essence, those,
Were yore days, but I didn't realize,
When my young face changed and,
I was that woman, who was once,
Found in the lanes of those taverns,
Where my childhood once belonged,

My eyes hold the pictures, of those,
Beautiful faces, those wore that cerise,
Red dot on their foreheads and that,
Prominent mark of vermillion depicting,
Their identity as woman, how I was,
So magnetically engrossed by them,
The simple cotton Taant sari that was,
Slight inches above their heels, of not,
Endorsing any style, simple yet elegant,
Even those creases sitting on yards nine,

Whole from the day's chore, I was a girl,
Then tender of age, yet my soul kept noticing,
All those images, whilst it was roving around,
Places, gazing on women merely, how,

It wanted to open those wings, waiting all,
These years for the journey to begin, from,
A girl to a woman, who has brought in dowry,
Lineage! Of an era that has gone by,
This lineage has become my arrogance,
How I feel it my obligation, to carry it on,

Over my shoulders, the tapestry of those hues,
The nine yards of history dying gradually,
I shall keep it going, that era which I have,
Lived by, that which my apprentice soul,
Took years waiting in disguise, to merge,
As one into my body, and now I can say,
With pride it has become part of me, that,
Which I am already living, into the mirror,
The Lineage I see is same, which time has,
Given me back, ti's a blessing being that woman...

Look Beyond

Have you seen behind!
Her eyes,
There is an ocean of salt,
Resting as tears,
Have you seen behind!
Her nostrils,
There you will find air,
Of toxic she breathes easy,
Have you seen behind!
Her lips,
There sits in silence myriad,
Unspoken words of despair,
Have you seen behind!
Her face,
There are hidden many layers of,
Emotions covered in disguise,
Have you seen behind!
Her neckline,
You will see how many times,
She has been choked,
Have you seen behind!
Her two shoulders,
You will see the load she carries,
But never complaint,
Have you seen behind!
Her bosoms,

You will find a bleeding heart,
That still pumps and seeks love,
Have you seen behind!
Her navel,
You will see the light residing,
Of life she has brought on earth,
Have you seen behind!
Her chastity,
You will see the pain of her,
Wounds inside closed like bud,
Have you seen behind!
Her thighs,
You will see she is more than flesh,
With marks of wounds from past,
Have you seen behind!
Her pair of knees,
You will find ache and cracks,
Still she stands firm on them,
Have you seen beneath?
Her bare feet,
You will see blood oozing red,
Pricked from the thorns of life,
Have you ever seen her soul naked?
Apart from her bare body,
Have you really seen her beyond?
Her body of flesh and curves,
She is more than that, she is a human...

Lover's Eyes

Smoke rising from the earthen stove,
Floating sky high, she blew air to the woods,
That came from her delicate lips, her eyes,
Irked yet with a smile she lit the first fire,
The smell of smoke, getting into nostrils,
Mine woke me, yet I slept like a child,

My ears alert to her morning ragas,
Followed the sounds of her silver anklet,
Even on my bed, I saw her divine beauty,
Loosening all the ducks and hens of coop,
As they quacked their way out in joy,
My sleep little disturbed, but wasn't I!

She with a smile, lifting the copper,
Pot moving like a swan, with her Alta,
Covered feet, walking to the pond with,
Grace, on time when the world slept,
Still dark outside, of early dawn mist,
Enjoyed her aloof bath, all sensuous and,

Wet! Her red bordered white sari,
Cladding tight to her skin, she quivers,
With the weight of her youth, leaving,

Terracotta Dreams

Behind the trail of her wet marks on,
The Ghats, she comes home holding,
The pot unto her waist, bunch of hibiscus,

In her fist, she offers to the Deity on way,
Waking all the gods, then wakes me up with,
Sprinkle of the Ganges, her wet tresses hold,
Awake to my senses though, I waited every day,
For her, to see her in wet sari, she was my,
Muse, my goddess and we held no ties,
Of man woman relationship, she agreed,
Upon this and I, and have lived and lived,
Long enough together, but people saw her,
With loathsome eyes, she wasn't bothered!
I never gave her vermillion, neither name,
A poet's heart I only wrote and wrote,

Verses myriad on her, Alas! Not my part,
Anymore, yet with wrinkled hands I,
Hold the pen, still with those lover's eyes,
I am writing poetry, aloof, alone in here,
The world despised our love, our bond,
No one understood ever was her lover I!

And she was mine,
She was solely mine!

Glossary

Alta A red dye which women in India especially Bengali and Oriya women in Eastern India apply with a cotton on the border of their feet.

Ghats A wide set of steps descending to a river

Macabre Love

When thy soul becomes rivulet,
Calm and soothing, my soul then,
Doesn't fear to float and drown,
Time and again, remaining beneath,
For long and yore, with wrinkles,
On the skin being soaked into,
Your wetness neither hurts nor,
Aches, yet seldom carried away by,
The ripples of your mind, the waves,
Oft! Pang me and shove me afar,
From where my soul awakes,
Soon gasping for air, feeling the,
Breathlessness, and my choking soul,
Struggles hard to swim and escape,
To the surface and be rescued again,
From the dismay of thy dark waters,
Why the same water then becomes,
Uncanny! Whilst that hand is again of,
Thy mercy, and yet again impelled,
To the bottom to drown one more time,
You want me to be sunken into,
You forever, like a soul in a rivulet,
Of love that flows from your heart,
Thy macabre love is it, I wonder must!

Marauding Eyes

As her girth rhymed with the gust,
She shivered and sauntered along,
Slightly cocooning beneath chiffon,
Struggling against cool gust her dusky,
Skin, she palpably needed warmth,
Of her beloved, far across he sat,
Refusing with ease he saw zilch,

Of her timid yet alluring gestures,
She kept gazing at his face with,
Dreams she was weaving in her head,
Of that moment, he caressingly filling her,
In his ample embrace, and she would,
Melt then all, forgetting the masquerade,
Emotions, and for once she thought,

How wonderful it would be to overlook,
The mayhem and evoke that lost love,
Desiring the seconds clogged and she,
Remains frozen inside his brawny arms,
And of course there was love, even in his,
Marauding eyes as he kept glancing,
From the corners of his twain,

Amid the horde of that unknown mob,
His gaze was solely upon her,

And visible on his fair face, was the truth,
How much was he taking delight!
Playing that game of hurting his pawn,
With silence, she seemed his effortless prey,
And he wanted to devour her leisurely...

Marijuana Life

There was some dust of life,
I found in the shallow abyss,
Handful of dust I filled in the bottle,
Brought some home to lie there,
In some void corner where no one,
Noticed, I had my life bottled,

Someone shook, a bottle full of dust,
Many emotions and feelings in that,
Shook along, then settled,
I fell, I rose, I cried, I laughed,
Again it was kept to lie,
In a corner, where if someone,
Noticed, I had my life bottled,

Alas! The dust had become I,
With time I aged and merged,
In water and sea, in streams of glee,
The surface was not the place,
I went deep and deeper,
Where no longer it affects,

The ripples do not touch me,
I feel glad that I am the dust,
I am it and it me,
I don't bleed anymore, I have no colour,

I have my life settled,
Where everyone noticed,

I have my life bottled,
Not with dust anymore,
With Marijuana, all smoke of reverie…

Maudlin Confessions

Sometimes I don't invite, but melancholia,
And maudlin arrives at my soul's dwelling,
Taking me back much back in time, where,
A better part of me is still lying quiet,
Seldom keeps my soul wandering there in,
The past lanes, to steal some moments from,
That little girl who still chirps and giggles,
Wearing those frocks which swirls to her,
Naive moves, she walks past me holding,
Her mother's a hand, a young beautiful lady,
In her thirties, I watch them disappear like,
A mute observer, whose lips are stitched,
I begged her once to give me some glee,
To take away with me, seemed I annoyed,
The little girl, and so I came back again,
Empty handed, it was her share not mine,
She without words pointed her finger,
And I looked behind, some blurred faces,
Perhaps the present for me, and her future,
She told me through her mute expressions,
Let me stay here forever, and touched my,
Heart, tears flowing from my eyes twain,
I couldn't bring any moment to lie in my,
Abode, and today standing in front of the,

Mirror as a woman, I have myriad emotions,
Locked inside my chest, and I make,
Hush confessions to the truth I noticed,
My reflection is still alike that little girl...

Melody of Maimed Heart

My heart is an ocean,
Where thy love lost ship,
Finds harbour, submerged,
In me are also myriad ships,
Loaded with burden,
Of emotions myriad,
Yet its vastness,
You can't hold in your eyes,
Neither in your cupped,
Palms for I shall wither away,
Leaving behind only the trails,
Of salt resting in your fist,
From the tears of many nights,
If shall you follow my silent,
Sobs you would see,
How much you had beaten,
My peaceful waters,
Creating ripples across,
Yet I had a heart of ocean,
And swallowed all,
Thy hurtful love,
Thine odious gape,
And it is still strange,
That never hath you!
Heard the melody that,
I sung oft, with a maimed heart...

Melting Desires

The nectar of love pouring,
Into thy soul and heart,
The doors of heavens open,
Into thine embrace of love,
My beloved, my arms wide,
Spreading and wrapping,
Thy bared body into mine,
Feeling the warmth of yours',
Sinking deep into the ocean,
Of melting desires!

Thine essence lingers on my soul,
Divine love touches inside,
Of all the nights and days,
Of all the winds and clouds,
Of all that is and that was,
I surrender my earthly body,
Unto your feet, my heart is a temple,
Thy soul resides, rising forever,
Are melting desires!

Thy, mine body is old, soul anew,
Leaping over into young bodies,
From flesh to ashes, flies time,
Benign Lord! Spare beloved's soul,

Fathom, our earthly love isn't over yet,
Twain bodies still burning in fire,
Embracing, merging, bathing,
In melting desires!

Moments Bygone

The darkness made us sightless,
To see our shadows still there,
Embracing and dancing to the,
Tunes of love, as we walked in,

Distance with annoyance eluding,
Each other's touch, yet our shadows,
Followed behind hand in hands,
Mingling and holding as tight,

We slept under one roof,
With backs turned, whilst!
Our shadows were locked in,
Each other's arms, making love,

They were black, dimness their dwelling,
With daylight they were murdered,
Short lived yet they spoke love,
Alas! Blessed with a corporeal body,

To make love, we never cared to notice,
And the night when you lit that,
Candle to have supper, sitting,
Afar with chairs seated athwart,

The shadows for first appeared,
Even when we quietly ate and gazed,
The two were busy kissing each other,
Reminding us those moments bygone,

We seemed much small in front of them,
They were giant shadows of us emitting,
Merely love and spreading more of it,
Ti's time it touched our hearts and core,

That night you sobbed and so did I,
Soon the shadows were us caught in real hold of love!

Morsels of Love

Slumbering noon's', the sun over high,
The head, bodies sweating in the light,
Running I came from an alien land,
Never liked the stay far from my home,
Three months seemed eternal and abiding,
In the midst of this chaos, she waited for me,
When the whole town was asleep,
Shutting down their doors till evening,
She remained awake, holding a plate full,
With lunch, a plate full of coastal meal,
She fed me with her hands bite by bite,
As I looked up to her face with keen eyes,
Her beautiful fair face still fresh inside me,
Back then it was only food, that finished,
Fast I wished, but today I have realized it was,
Her sheer care, my mother's handfed morsels of love...

Musings of a Beloved

Thy love is seductive, like the crimson,
Hued horizon, where souls our dance,
In the joy of earthly love, the spilling desires,
On the floor, are like wet dew drops on,
The mowed grass of dawn's cascading arrival,

Thy touch is like sedative, soothes soul mine,
The fingers when dance on my dusky skin,
Ecstasy blooms and dances through my silken gown,
The warmth of your fair skin embracing mine,
Is like twain soul burning in fire of flesh within,

Thy kissing is fragrant, lingers long inside me,
And my essence then merges with yours,
Locks of eternity it seems, the wetness like of,
Fresh jasmine buds and tuberose seals love,
Ours, on lips of both, as it ends with a smile,

Thine embrace is like sanctuary, from the mayhem,
Of my own impish thoughts, I oft take refuge,
As you stand with thy broad chest, taking,
Chaos to go through you, as I stand hidden in the,
Rear of your shadow, thy love is more than making
love!

Yes! These are the musings of thy confined beloved,
From the rambling corners of her unspoken words...

***

Musings of a Beloved II

Tonight I want to fall in love,
All over again, holding thy hands,
Leaning over you, I want you to,
Kiss me for once and forever,
I know time shall not cease,
And before I seal my eyes in,
Deep slumber of eternity,
Let me for once and all, see thy,
Face cupped in my hands,
Let me smell thy manly elixir,
That's all over my bare body,
When the sheets were craggy,
And nights were long,
Even the dawn took consent,
To arrive at our doorway,
I Shall not be ever again this,
Beauty in thine arms, let me,
For once again tell you, before,
I am dust and my skin is creased,
I have loved you ferociously,
Perchance! if you ever noticed,
Whilst standing on the edge of life,
My eyes longed thy sight, and my,
Dusky skin thy warmth, embrace me,
Fill me within thy wide coffer, for I,
Still am yearning for thou to be mine,

And I as thy beloved, alas! When the,
Time would cease, for last I'll kiss thy,
Lips much harder and let my essence,
Reside in thy soul forever!

Yes! These are the musings of thy prosaic beloved,
From the rambling corners of her unspoken heart...

Nights of Romance

Arms across my body, a whisper in my ears,
Noises in the air, and the words disappeared,
The fog making it blurred, that face not visible,
A male figurine behind the smoke, presumed I,
The closer I went, the shadow appeared lost,
The distance didn't seemed to finish this time,

Something pulled my body, strongly towards,
My heart longing to see the face, someone known,
Long known from my past, I dared go ahead,
Couldn't with feet jammed, my whole body tied,
I felt he stood there somewhere, gazing me weak,
Choking, struggling, I wanted to give up,

When someone lifted my whole body,
Way up high, I felt I could fly that moment,
I touched the sky, the night touching mine,
Piercing within me, I stood only skin,
Beautiful! I saw my soul,
Beautiful! I saw his soul,

Ah! I saw him for the first, not a stranger,
His arms inviting, I ran wild to get that warmth,
It felt much known, that touch, that breath,
He made love to me, my whole body swirling,

Terracotta Dreams

Like a doll in his arms, I wanted to be there,
Forever! Desiring, hoping that night to freeze,

He slowly whispered in me, words clear,
It was time to wake up! A slight throw,
On the bed, my eyes opened to see the darkness,
That still captured the room, my heart broke,
Into pieces, I realized again I was so alone,
My hands touching that hollow side of bed,

When I knew I had him, now it's just memories,
Of him, that comes knocking into my dreams,
Night after night, sadly the days are passing by,
I miss those nights of romance, those nights,
Of passionate love making, his camaraderie,
Seldom in this alley, is my eyes wide awake!

Trying to find those missing pieces of nights,
Trying to find those nights filled with our romance...

Nine Yards of Love
(Part One)

Her eyes open with his pleading,
"Moina...Tea"!
She wakes up in haste and rushes to,
The mud and dung covered stove,
She puts the water in a pan and,
Applies her Bindi, in the middle of,
Her brows carefully, with the clear,
Water bubbling in the pan, she ties
Her long tresses in a rough bun,
She then rushes to the wooden,
Cabinet takes out the sugar,
Tea leafs and pours them all in,
She then tucks the sari's pallu,
To her fair belly within the petticoat,
And covers her blouse with another,
End of her sari, rushing then to the,
Goat tied outside her kachcha kitchen,
Milking some fresh creamy milk,
For her husband's hot tea,
The liquor has spread in the air,
Filling his nostrils with essence of tea,
And he calls one more time,
In a mellow voice, "Moina",
And she then comes walking,

To their sleeping room, hands
Over the tea, and he sips it making,
Loud noises in seconds one or two,
Tea is not what he is waiting,
It's her radiant face he wants to,
See, and all that she does every day,
In the kitchen to look beautiful,
He pulls one end of the pallu,
Lovingly and caressingly,
And she blushes like a new bride,
His love has been festive evermore,
And days like rejoice, she partakes,
The joy of looking beautiful,
To her lover's eyes!
And graceful even in her homely,
Seem, those nine yards are sign,
Of his eternal and sane love,
She wraps them merrily around,
Her body and he take pride,
When she walks by his side, As his soul mate and bride!

Continued...

Glossary

Nine Yards full length of the longest traditional sari
Kachcha Made of mud, straw and dry leaves
Pallu the Loose end of a Sari
Bindi A decorative mark worn in the middle of the forehead by Indian women, especially Hindus.

Nine Yards of Pride
(Part Two)

"Look Moina I have something for you,"
He cajoled, with a devilish beam,
Oh his face, she read and blushed,
Standing slight far in the doorway,
With a lopsided smile,
She came closer and whispered into his,
Ears, "I know what it is",
He glanced and she did same,
Their eyes met and desires danced,
Within their youthful hearts,
He grinned and gave the brown,
Paper package, "wear this tonight!"
She nodded and snatched,
Ran away with giggles and joy,
Went to her dressing room,
Staring at own reflection in the,
Mirror, the curls of hair falling,
Over her temple, and fair cheeks,
Blushing without applied hues,
She threw the wrinkled garment,
From her body, of the days',
Errand and hum drum of life,
There was no time to be wasted,
To fold the clothes and keep,

Them neatly on the wooden,
Cloth holder, desires will,
Neither wait nor her youth,
The whole day went otherwise,
Doing house hold chores and more!
The feelings arising now,
Seemed magnetic and much,
Thunderous to shy away,
Rising inside her body like,
Waves of ecstasy!
Her whole youthful flesh
Vibrating in glee, tearing callously,
The packet her eyes twinkled,
Lips smiled in glee,
A green south silk with,
Broad border and motifs,
She wrapped it around her,
Body roughly, her bare shoulders,
Revealing, along with her back,
She combed her hair in a bun,
Adorning them with sweet-smelling, Jasmines from
her garden,
Treading slow the hallway,
Holding her gorgeous Silk Sari,
She came inside the mammoth,
Room where he was,
Waiting much eager,
Turned his face with the,
Sounds of her silver anklet,
His eyes widened to see,
His bride wrapped in nine yards,

And his heart again felt the,
Pride and kismet to have her,
As his wedded companion for life...

Continued...

Nine Yards of Twinge
(Part Three)

Time was the cruellest that year,
How it faded and slipped,
Through the fingers of his,
Wrinkled hands like sand,
Moina was resting on her death,
Bed, he despised her now and,
Said, "You cheated me, you,
Said a lie, your promises are,
Fake, why you did to me when,
You couldn't keep!" the old,
Husband now cries in his,
Aloofness, they were lovers,
Of an era which had bygone,
The reminiscences are now strong,
She meekly stared, but replied none,
Words have long stopped coming,
It was her eyes that spoke,
She was still beautiful in his eyes,
A young beautiful bride wearing,
Nine yards of alluring silks,
Those views are fresh, when,
She had filled the house with,
Mirth making it alive with her,
Chirping and vigorous gestures,

Wrapped evermore in saris,
Now he held her hand more oft,
To express his incessant love,
Alas! One dawn was ghastly,
A man who was mute mostly,
And silent towards the world,
Woke the heavens that day,
When his wife closed her eyes,
His sobs were heard till far, and to,
The farthest lands where they,
Had travelled together on foot,
How glorious was that time, when,
Their love was praised and ogled,
He has protected his Moina for long,
From every harm, but this time,
He was the loser in the God's house,
He stood alone, all by himself,
Slowly the mob going homes,
He watched the deviant fire gulp,
Her earthly body in hours few,
Like a python it seemed that night, Fetching on its
prey, he was never,
Alone in walking home, she had,
Walked along matching every step,
Making him feel the pride more,
Now the house is hollow, who shall?
There wait in those pretty saris,
And the ringing anklet that filled the,
House with her presence, he wished,
To die that night, coming back,
For first in many years, he opened,
Her wooden almirah, next to that,

Mud made kitchen, a small room,
Where she wore those nine yards of,
His love, he saw them in the lantern,
Light, hanging neatly still holding,
That shine, he rubbed his hands over,
Them and tears began rolling,
Who will wear these now?
Who will give me that tea?
The nine yards of her benign presence,
Into his life and her absence going,
To be long now was the deviant twinge...

End

One Fistful of Glee

In the mediocre of that unspoken space,
Where she exist, and there are many faces,
In the mirror, but she saw herself as one,
And in everyone, she sold her soul,
Sold her conscience, was it all worth the game?

In those red bangles in her hand,
Even the might of the sun was caged,
They turned red reflecting through,
The cool glass bangles settled on her hands till,
She was lost in the crowd of so many,

Serious and calm faces, she wondered,
They all looked same, she found herself,
In the giggles of young girls, in the newly married,
Brides' smile, in the mute words of mid life,
And in the calmness of those wrinkles,
She found the story in all of them, she found it same,

She kept shouting in the crowd of a mute world
Shed off those clothes of pride, shed off that fake smile,
For once let your naked soul be revealed,
See me, see me, am I the same you saw me?
Feel me, feel me, am I the same you knew me?
Not what I was! I already sold my soul,

She did it long back; like them like many,
Murdered but not dead, beaten but not shaken,
They all know the path to their happiness,
And now does she, she knows what it takes,
To get one fistful of love,
To get one fistful of glee!

Paradise Waiting

In the mirage of a dreamy world,
There was a wanderer with thirst of love,
He walked and walked miles,
To reach his beloved, the abode in dark,
That stands silently beneath the starry sky,
And the smoke rising from the chimney,

Grabbed his eyes from afar, bare feet,
He walks upon earth, thorns and stones,
Pricking feet, nothing stops him tonight,
His queen is waiting in her poor hut,
With torn sheets and kaput roof,
The smoke rising from water cooking,

In the pot, the signal she sends tonight,
He comes meddling the woods and night,
Crossing low rivers, pebbles and mud,
Hastily stepping the barriers of world,
His heart longs to be one and,
To make love, sink deep into her soul,

And he reaches falling, treading,
Meadows and dung's, dust covers,
The clothes and his strong male body,
Unstoppable and careless he stands bare,

She embraces him, their bodies entwined,
Desires slowly unfolding of love, of ardour,

Tonight is their last, by dawn they shall,
Be gone forever, leaving behind memories,
Of bodily love, of passion, the world is,
Not the place to be, their love is beyond,
The man made walls and derelicts,
Have blocked them from bodily unison,

For them now the gates are open, paradise is waiting,
The gates have opened, to homage forever their bodily
love...

Parijatha's Soliloquy

Her braid long snake like reaching till loins,
Hung on bare back of hers, she is dusky skin,
She plucked me from her garden, I shied,
With love she adorned her braid besetting me,
I blossomed more in pride, filling her tresses,
With aroma mine so fine, timid yet vigorous,
She waited for someone tonight, calmly on bed,

The hearth dark, dimly lit with lantern light,
I saw him come, dark toned tall strong body,
Carved muscles of a peasant's hand, he was wet,
All sweat with his body filled with manly odour,
He stood in his dirt stained loincloth, bare coffer,
Keeping his plough on earth he glanced quietly,
At her, who was all and so was he aroused high,

Pouncing over her wild yet gentle, it was pure love,
Loosened her braid, her khadi attire wasn't a barrier,
I fell on her bosom, on her heart, hearing the beats,
That said his name; I wanted to be there forever,
But soon his hands crushed me, I bled in pain,
And more and more I was all pressed harder,
A soft tender flower, I admired now myself more,

Between twain bare lovers no breeze shall pass,
Heavenly love of warm bodies, I saw it all,

I had lost myself into them, I have been trodden,
Into their making love, lying beside them pondered,
What beautiful unison of man and woman!
To this I felt pride, pride of being lover's delight,
And gave fine essence till I breathed my last,

My blood had no colour; my pain had no sound,
Still even I love her heart, with dawn she again,
Picked me from earth, my soul still aromatic,
I have given love mark, last night my saffron hue,
On heart her's, she love me too, making a rough bun,
Smiled, once again putting my corpse on her tresses!
And ti's divine soliloquy is Parijatha's told tale...

Glossary

Parijatha Night flowering coral jasmine

Pilgrimage

There is a chasm of tears,
My soul often! Visits,
Without arousing,
The corporeal body,
Leaves in hushed,
Murmurs, a casement,
Remains ever unbolt,
Enters my soul there,
Without taking me,

It keeps probing for,
Something in those,
Kaput pieces of past,
That penetrated deep,
In my body, with bruises,
Still resting as marks,
They said the tears,
Would heal, and so my,
Soul wants to steal,

Few droplets filled,
In that chasm flowing,
As rivulet, innocence,
Doesn't make it see,
Those tears are mine,
When in days yore,

I paid pilgrimage to that,
Door where mayhem,
Was my mate!

And to sluice the twinge,
Purge and cleanse,
Burden that grave,
I seldom kept going,
To the pilgrimage in solace,
My soul yet trapped,
Doesn't know the salt,
From tear's rivulet shall,
Blaze my flesh of past wounds,

Even the sanctity of pilgrimage,
Won't heal, perhaps till I breathe...

Possessive

I fell from the tree,
Dropped from heavens,
Into thy lap,
I was never born,
I had no dwelling,
Where I belonged!
Moulded this mud doll,
To be loved,
Solely by you,
They gave me no heart,
That would beat for,
Them as well, no mother,
No father, I had no,
Possession left behind,
Living in this void,
To be loved,
Barely by yours,
Possessive love,
And you still enjoyed,
Listening to that amorous song,
Playing it again and again...

Reflection

A simple low-priced cotton sari,
A stitched blouse to match with,
Hair neatly made into bun,
A round red bindi on the forehead,
A voluptuous figurine and fairly tall,
Accessories too contemporary that fall,
Matching with the sari wrapped,
Elegantly, it was the reflection of,
Myriad women on the mirror who,
Stood tall, beside their men, my mother,
And aunts, I have seen them all,
And now I follow into their,
Footsteps and feel proud of them all,
The legacy of gracious Indian,
Womanhood continues with me,
And shall with,
Many alike of our reflections...

Glossary

Bindi A colourful dot worn in the middle of the forehead by Indian women.

Rhapsody of the Contract

A wagon of clouds passing by, hopped in soul my,
With a piece of paper, the sole passenger was I,
Crossing the oceans and rivers, passed by the highs,
Topsy- turvy, whirling and the engine bellowing,
One look at the paper I held it tight in my fist,
First stop, the platform of night!
Squeaked the wheels on the invisible tracks,

Jumped out I, and asked why? Why that paper?
A golden one with signature mine,
The night replied with bewildered eyes,
Hail to the stars, journey to the constellations,
Perhaps then, thy question shall be answered,
The wagon bellowed again, and ran I,
This time to the stars, with hope in eyes,

Only hopes, no sleep, the cost was too high,
A sparkling trail it followed, nothing less,
Than paradise, next stop the galaxies to stars!
Bewildered I felt with so many, saw one shining bright,
The wagon read my mind; it took me to the one,
I cried from inside, "What the golden paper have I?"
An unknown quest, I was the traveller in time,
The brightest one smiled and smiled,

Pointing me towards the North, replied,
"Thy soul shall travel to a bright light, till the end,
For I am not the brightest or the mightiest,"
Wagon throwing steams of clouds ran again,
Moving this time faster, the last stop to reach by,
I shall have all my answers then, oh! Poor curious
mind,
Soon huge vast golden gates came to my sight,

Eyes became blind; the words of the bright one rang,
The gates were open, the wagon disappeared,
Perhaps! It was the final destination for me to arrive,
A voice echoed, "shall you cometh, ti's my will,
Shall you do, ti's my will, is it too much a price?"
Soon woke up on my bed, with a little sleep had I,

Realized what my quest in time is about,
Had made a contract, before was I born,
It's now time to walk the path, sleep was,
A tiny price to pay, a fair gain on my side,
Rhapsody I partake, the agreement is a blessing,
With no expiration date, perhaps I know now, who!
Made that golden contract and I am a writer, I write…

Rose's Tale of Love

Autumn at its fullest, spreading over the trees,
Deciduous are shedding a fast their maturity,
Coming off their old torn clothes, they'd worn long,
Waiting for the spring to arrive again in their hearts,
Ah! What a sight of both severance and patience,
Unlike its sister, autumn is bare yet prides on its beauty,

Pride for a reason, hidden by many even the fall knew
not,
There was a bush of thorns standing in solace,
Hiding its beloved, a beautiful rose white like snow,
Velvety its body and delicate as dandelions puff,
 But her beauty was not something he could hide!
For long, and when she blossomed at her fullest,

Her mystical fragrance spread, on the wings of wind,
Bringing along many to witness the youthful white
rose,
She was praised, ah! She was praised for her beauty,
With every admiring compliment she got, she blushed,
And she blushed! Every time evolving red,
Her petals from white, into the marvellous colour of
love,
The words of praising came and came, turning her red,

Ah! She had become this alluring red rose, red like
blood,
Alas! Her possessive lover the mighty bush of thorns,
Couldn't control his rage, sightless in ego and pride,
Pricked her heart with his thorns, embracing her,
Hard in his barbed cloak, made her bled, turning her,
Again into a white rose from red, her pain was visible,
Her white body was covered with strains of blood,

The white rose loved the thorns more than her,
She was born into it, so shall die into his arms,
Oh! So fragile her petals fell on earth, he saw,
With tearful eyes, and now are gone all the ones,
Who praised! For there was nothing that pleased their
eyes,
The thorny bush now stands alone, aloof, amid the
barrenness,
Holding rose's tale of love, his own tale in his weeping
heart,

Gone are the breezes of autumn that kept flowing,
Gone are the humming birds, wishing to drink her
nectar,
When she was alive, ah! When she was alive!
He understood never, what she brought was life,
Into that fall, when no flowers dared to blossom,
 Poor! He couldn't keep her, protect her, but killed her,
With his gruesome act of possessiveness, he stands
culprit,

All he has now are her dried petals; he keeps close to heart,
All he has now are her dried petals; he keeps close to heart ...

Glossary

Fall Autumn Season

Saint or the Sinner

You looked at me once and said, "Darling"!
I shall be back, wait for me tonight,"
I bid you farewell, with mute words,
And speaking eyes, I didn't liked the,
Parting and your gestures told the same,
You turned twice again with loving eyes,

I was sitting in the chariot of love,
Watching you distancing gradually from,
Me and my heart, the pang was thunderous,
Just alike the lightening that frightened,
Many times, I shivered in my aloofness,
Glancing you becoming shadow in the rain,

You seemed farther now, my eyes,
Could see, in the dark twilight with,
The sounds of peter- patter growing loud,
The army of droplets falling over the,
Roof and dripping through the panes,
With shadows unknown passing by,

My heart waited thine arrival and sight,
Time was running ahead of me, the clock,
Churned faster that night, my eyelids heavy,
With last sleep, and I was about to fall,

On the velvet seat, slowly my head tilting,
Down, my eyelids fighting hard to see,

Your face one last time, a tear rolled down,
My cheeks, I was falling in an abyss dark,
As raven, when sudden jerk came and held,
My hands, the chariot door opened and I,
Saw you calling my name, "Darling come,"
And I was saved from the doom that almost,

Fetched my soul tonight, I was still alive,
And I stood out, hopped under the umbrella,
That you were standing with to save me from,
Incessant rain, little do you know dear! You,
Saved me from going there, where I could,
Never see your face, how rude the rain played,
On me, was it the saint or the sinner tonight?
But it did melted the distance between us,
As you held me by shoulders to keep me safe...

Seductive Irreversible Sins

Night sky adorned with stars, watching silently,
Waves wearing white cloak, splashed gently,
Kissing the shore with her wet and salted lips,
He was waiting, for her the whole day and life,
Burning every day in the dawn, Oh! Villainous sun,
The nature thought, the heavens and the creatures too,
There was no man on earth, who could love such,

With such vigour and insanity, his beloved with pain,
Chaotic and surrealism mantras only chanted by men,
But the nature forgot that vicious apple created though,
Forbidden, yet eaten by the man and the woman,
The seductive love had arisen, bare bodies were,
Walking the earth, falling in love with their opposites,
Then the sinful saga began, and still continues same,

Twin flames were reciprocating the seductive love,
Bind in oneness, the souls were touched in fusion,
Every earthly female and male body was speaking love,
The lustful, sinful, divine yet capricious gestures,
Was spreading like a spate in all directions across,
This love was defied, oh! So defied by the gods,
Alas! They created, distractions and rules of oneness,

Broken, written were new rules in the heaven's sacred
book,
The men's heart shall beat for two, seduced by many,
Their love couldn't by pious than nature's eternal love,
Woman shall bring love, so shall she befall the curse,
Of seductive irreversible sins in love to be committed,
By one and many, time and again the sin has to be,
Made, the walls of chaste love has to be wrecked,

The lovers and the beloved needs be abandoned,
Need be in aloofness, and so thy God created sins of
love,
And created the potion, hid it in the hearts seen by only
those,
Who came back to home, to their true soul mate!
The one who would be his twin flame in the journey
to be,
And those hearts which passed the test, would be,
The twin flames of eternity, their souls together till
infinity,

Ah! Thus, the love of lust became the love of burning
hearts,
Ah! Thus, the love of sins became the love of two souls
in fire

Seeing My Older Self from the Eyes of My Younger Self

That dusk was an ordinary one,
The twilight inflowing silently,
Leisurely embracing my galleria,
And the twittering of flocks of birds,
In the saffron sky, returning to their,
Nests, a droplet of sweat dripped by,
Of the summer's dusk, from my,
Cheeks reminding me of the time,
I sauntered towards my kitchenette,
Brewed the leaves in boiling water,
Seeing it turning red, the liquor was,
Released, and I kept staring from the,
Casement while making the tea,
Pouring it then carefully into the,
Pot, resting it beside a plate full of
My homemade fresh Chocó cookies,
Yes! I was generous enough to pour the,
Chocolate chips in it, and sizing them,
Giant, one shall fill the hunger of my,
Beloved, who'll be home any sooner!
Before the twilight breaks and night,

Awakes from its day's long slumber,
I have to serve him tea, but before his,
Arrival I have to get ready, adorn my grey,
Hair with jasmines, taking one glance,
At my wrinkled, yet beautiful face,
That kohl of youthful days still rests,
On my weary eyes, and lips have turned,
Naturally blue, showing the frost taking,
Over, gladly we are still in much love,
As seeing each other's face after a day,
Long of chores, the enthusiasm remains the,
Same, of those youthful days, I often wonder,
How time fled, seeing my man growing,
Old and he saw me slowly getting wrapped,
Beneath the sheets of wrinkles, we have,
Been fortunate, to be still each other's side,
I was soon then ready in my small,
Garden with a tea pot, cups and cookies,
And I must tell, that I have heard words,
Echoing in air, as the aroma fled,
On the chariot of gust, myriad mouths,
Were willing to taste that tea, made with,
Love, but it was solely for him to have,
In these few of our numbered years,
Goodness! Then I saw his silhouette,
Standing as a shadow, as he approached,
He had a warm smile, and we did drank in,
Peace, from those cups of love, but coming,
Till here was a journey, of lows and highs,
That we overcame together as man and wife,
I wish and eye this life for my older self,

Beside my lover, how much my younger self,
Humbly wishes! This waiting shall never,
Stop and neither shall those tea cups,
Ever remain hollow, it'll be the end then...

Still There

The clay from the Ganges, shaped like a doll,
Cooked in fire long, as I sat and watched it all,
Turned red from brown, and paper dress on,
It had no pretty face, no fancy hair or clips,
Two hands stretched immovable, two legs,
Just a human figure it was all! Yet I played,
Long and long, for hours and more,
She made it for me with love, my aunt,
Sitting on the mud and dung plastered porch,
Near the pond, where few ducks quacked,
Time and again, swimming and floating,
On the green waters, covered with moss,
It was a different world, a different place then,
Those hands wrinkled, eyes blurred now,
Those mud made dolls are lost somewhere,
No long I get to hear the quacks anymore,
In the urban, yet I find myself wandering,
Alone on wheels of life, sitting beside my soul,
In the times left behind, and the places,
Lived once, it seems I have come afar,
Yet some part of me remains still there,
And silently watches that little girl and her,
Aunt talking, playing and laughing,
While making those clay dolls with hands,
Their hands all covered in clay, and now I,
Don't like to play, it irks to get hands dirty,

The doll had been cooked in fire, or was it me?
Was it my soul getting cooked to face mellowness?
A part of me longs but to go there, much hollow here,
And they are still there, in that small mud house,
Alas! But not me,
Alas! But not me...

Sulking Love

What about those marauding eyes?
They almost and often ate my soul,
I was lying half dead already, within,
My corporeal body, barely breathing,
Yet longing for thy love, thy romance,

The crime wasn't fatal, but the confines,
You made with barbs of the connubial,
Ties pierced me deep inside, I was to,
Depart this earth, my vision slight blurred,
I only saw a deviant face, hidden beneath,

That wandered hitherto, surrounding,
My vulnerable soul, and my beats,
Swift, did I ever told you, I tasted blood,
That oozed upwards, from my own heart,
Yet I kept yearning for thy sulking love...

Sweet Conspirer

The word travelled on the orifice,
Of sinuous gust and was taken,
Far across the maze of clouds,
To the heaven and spoken,
In hushed words, to the ears of,
The golden robed and roared he,
With a thunder, his words,
Became the lightening,
The gust dreaded but smiled,
Aghast! Exiled from the gates,
Fell the gust upon earth,
And whispered in the ears of,
Twain earthly lovers!
The message from the heavens,
As the two still lost in the,
Bottomless slumber of mayhem,
With tears dried on the sides,
Of their closed eyes,
A forbidden truth revealed,
For rescuing that fallen love,
Whose pieces were lying tattered!
On the floor of their hearts,
"They had decreed the command,
The bond is forever and beyond,
Which thy souls have signed,
Before thy human avatar,

Came into the womb for nine,
And so shall it be fulfilled,"
The gust told all, and fled from,
The casement, filling their,
Hearth and their hearts,
With the golden truth,
And no sooner they rose from,
The divan, gathered all the,
Pieces of their ruined hearts,
And the sweet conspirer gazed,
From behind the casement,
In between blowing the curtains,
That rose and fell, soothing their skin,
And arouse as well, some emotions,
From past, the love filled days and,
The lovers ran and embraced each other,
The gust now couldn't pass from between,
Their earthly bodies, wrapped in making love,
And thus it smiled seeing the love,
Of twain souls reviving,
Covered for long, in their dust of ego...

Tears

Wrapped in white sheets on his death bed,
An unknown man, lifeless, breathless!
Soon got lifted his body from earth to be taken away,
Resting on shoulders four, as they chanted,
God's name, his wife sitting beside for last,
Sobbing in grief, and stood I gazing little from far,
Couldn't come closer by!
Couldn't watch to see her cry!
Too much pain pricked my heart and more,
The view of a dead body lifted from earth,
Stirred the deepest emotions in me,
Tears began flowing from my eyes,
Yes even I cried, and his eyes too,
I gazed across the mob, staring at his red face
My beloved a strong man, still he cried,
He stood there little afar, yet our eyes met,
And shared we some silent words, he felt,
And so did I, an uncanny feeling wrapped us,
To see that stranger's body taken away,
Made us cry, it felt not was he taken,
But it was something of ours'!
He was no one but gave us the lesson of love,
Coming back I was in my mate's embrace,
For longer time, tears flowing myriad
From eyes of both, and souls of both,
Dust to dust, womb to tomb it all was!

That dead man gave us back, what we had,
Lost in time, I didn't realized when he cleansed,
Our souls and we read the hidden message
In the air, and shed many tears over his grave...

Terracotta Dreams

The virgin drop of heaven's water,
On parched land of my soul,
Quenched my thirst of inner desires,
I was bearing the fissure for long,
My soul was set to be moulded,
On the wheels of the veiled potter,
And be baked and burnt in the,
Fire of his mammoth sized oven,
Where my eyes saw one after other,
He altered myriad beings of passion,
Giving shapes to their dreams,
Putting them into human moulds,
And I loved the essence too of my,
Earthen soul burning in the fire,
Of maudlin moods, some glee along,
And taking shape into earthen vessel,
That shall hold prose and verses,
Transforming red, the cracks got filled,
With the fire of passion from heaven's
Resistant on the facade yet,
Fragile from inside, lingering fresh,
Spreading farther the smell of my,
Soul much alike the petrichor,
Wet and soaked, my terracotta dreams...

That Known Face

Wandering in the desert of the man,
Once lost forever, carrying much baggage,
Of life, a suitcase filled with emotions,
A trunk full of melancholia, alas! Lost,
My baggage holding glee, in the host,
Looking for it soul mine, ubiquitously,

In the midst of storm, midst of chaos,
There were myriad standing, I glanced,
Like me, feet chained to their baggage,
Of gloominess, annoyance and tears,
Spilling over, they stood like puppets,
Immovable, I shook them but in vain,

They chose to sleep in deep slumber of,
Eternal grief, not I! Oh not I!
So I went to the scrap collector once,
My trunk filled with cynicism, to sell,
Them all, the weight all from my soul,
Oh! Poor me he wasn't the buyer of those,
And so I found none, yet in the midst,

Of my sordid times, I saw one face,
A familiar stranger, and every face was his,
All seemed my lover's visage, I grew even more,
Forlorn, he was everywhere around me,

His voice echoing in my ears, his,
Shadow following mine, I saw him,
I heard him, delirium of my soul perhaps,

Perchance pure love of lovers us, agape!
In the end I found him in the mausoleum,
In the times of mayhem, Oh yes! He was,
My saviour, he was the soul magpie,
Collected every wretched corner of my,
Soul, making it a new, I had always loved,
Him, that known face, that known stranger,
Who were both, the sinner and the healer!

The Abyss

I was there sitting on the ruined chair,
Stitching the torn pieces of my heart,
You knew I had only one, yet you pierced,
And pricked time and again, my beloved,
I have bled a lot before; I had bled in red,
I know some pieces are lost but I managed,
Stitching it with few torn pieces of cloth,

I made big loops of thread so that you see,
I am broken inside out, so that you hear,
I am still giving beats, and those for you,
You stabbed me myriad times with words,
All like thorns, harsh and ripped my skin,
And yet I had the heart to love you again,

This time I lit some more candles of love,
Into the abyss you pushed me in and left,
The light was dim; I barely saw your face,
But knew you were there, loving with loathe,
My soul and more, and to make you sure,
That I still suffered, yes I felt pain of yore,

I wrapped my heart into the wire of thorns,
And walked around with feet chained in iron,
I made noise of locks clinking, whilst moving,

And oozed blood so that you smelled the hurt,
Alas! The abyss is now my home, and I am afraid,
To fly out alone, you have cut my wings of dare...

The Bed Tea

The curtains are dark, they impede the light,
From dawn's virgin ray to fall on my eyes,

My space is silent ever, it swallows noises,
From the world outside, nothing disturbs,

My sweet slumber of winter's warmth,
Beneath the duvet, not even the birds,

Wake me up to their chirps and tweets,
But only my beloved's much manly voice,

He wakes me calling my name in his,
Sweet yet egoistic manner, his day begins,

With my made cup of tea, hot and steaming,
And even I won't deny, I enjoy his thud,

In my ears, the love filled pleading,
As he sits waiting inside the duvet yet warm,

And I walk to the kingdom of utensils,
Reflecting my face on them, half sleepy half awake,

As I still wrestle to find the pot from shelf,
And he enjoys hearing the clashing of steel,

It tells him of my presence in kitchen and life his,
Ever he waits patiently for me to arrive with a tray,

Holding two giant mugs and some cookies,
This has become the first raga of our mornings'

For years, to smell the aroma that fills our little,
Hearth with my made cup of his perfect bed tea!

The Bride (Part One)

Her body was covered in eclectic,
Attire with twinkles myriad that,
Came from the skies, to embellish,
Her beautiful fair skin, she beamed in,
Night, the sky was her mate, she was,
Getting married to the son of God!

The azure sky was roaring tonight,
Expressing his manhood to the clouds,
And stars, commanding them to go,
To his new bride and adorn her with,
Beautiful blossoms and not fine clothes,
For there no need of such earthly things,

In his vast abode, his kingdom was pious,
And divine, with eyes eighteen and ears nine,
The planets gave their words, they shall,
Never break the confines, of his merrily,
Abode when the sky's new bride arrives,
Ah! She was a woman, beautiful, youthful,

The night came, and the chariot of 'Sky',
Arrived on the facade of her small dwelling,
Where once he saw her singing the songs,
Of her hymen, her melodious voice went,

Till heavens and the seven skies, and the,
Youngest of them all, the first sky above earth,

Gave away his heart to this earthly woman,
With lightening his chariot arrived and,
Commanded he, I shall marry you from,
Nine days now, be ready you shall be mine,
The young woman in awe, uttered no word,
And the youngest and the mightiest fled,

And merged in night, she had no say! Came,
The day ninth, but the night his mistress took,
Away all its stars and made the darkest,
Night, the younger groom now threw thunder,
Showing its anger and it rained; the bride,
Drenched, her tears of dismay too merged in same,

Damped and cold, shivering and timid,
She came into her new dwelling, there,
Was no bed, no hearth no mirth, merely,
He and his vast reign of sky, she sobbed,
For months and days many and it rained,
And rained incessantly, he cared never,

Roving in kingdom his, on chariot of clouds,
Came to her with ardent desires, made,
Love to her day and night and she remained,
A gloomy bride, with no happiness and pride,
In her heart to keep, but with time she fell in,
Love, ah! At last she fell in love with him,

Her handsome husband, the youngest of,
The sky and the kingdom filled with,
Laughter and glee, they two spent time,
In each other's arms, lost in their brief,
Love life, the son of God forgot she was,
An earthly woman he married, her body was,

Fated to die, and how the ages passed,
Away, and the bride now lying on her,
Death bed, took his hand into her's,
Leaving her earthly body forever, that day,
The sky cried and there was thunderstorm,
The whole night, Alas! Their wedlock ended,

With her demise, he sat with her dead body,
In his lap and cried, tears turned into rain,
The earth flooding with water everywhere,
And he cursed himself now for being a God,
A God with dismay and an eternal life,
What was to do with his powers and pride?

His vast kingdom and clouds infinite,
Alas! He could not keep her body forever,
Neither could he conjure his beautiful bride,
Yes! He cursed himself for being a 'God',
That incessant life of his, he loathed,
This twinge was much for him to bear as a man...

Continued...

The Bride (Part Two)

Alas! His God ship seemed like a curse,
He walked upon earth treading those,
Places time and again where the two,
Had spent hours of love and togetherness,
And the nymphs and muses all glanced,
In vehemence, they ogled and all giggled,

Swishing the boughs and sitting on the,
Chariot of zephyr they oft troubled his,
Coveted peace, their aroma so fine and,
Alluring he smelt and knew they were,
The heavenly nymphs in their heavenly,
Lucid attires, expressing more of their,

Feminine aura to win his heart one more,
Time, yet the youngest of the sky was in,
Love with his earthly woman, whose carcass,
He had kept safe in a glass casket, he was,
Filled with anger again, for so many years,
He has not roared, hasn't shown his valour,

The new bride of his, taught him love,
Made him calm, which the nymphs broke,
They aroused his rage; he now rode on his,
Stallion of clouds, the immortal god was,

Revengeful towards the heaven's conspiracy,
He came to his abode, picked up the lock,

To the casket and took out his new bride's
Carcass, adorning once again into red his,
Wife, pierced the dagger into his heart,
He took the blood oozing from his still,
Beating heart, filling it again on her forehead,
He granted her a new life, but broke the,

Forbidden rule of the paradise, to give own,
Life to conjure a human from the realm,
Of the dead, than shall his soul will rot,
Forever there for the rest of his eternal life,
The bride opened her eyes to see the face,
Of her beloved, and ran into his embrace,

Alas! A horrid chariot, made with cadaver,
And skulls, was rounding in their reign,
He told her all, the forbidden rule and,
Now he was to be the prisoner in hell,
Her tears turned into a brook, she held,
His hand firmly not to let him go ever,

Alas! Too late the black robed figure,
Came close, dragged her husband with,
An uncanny force, she had no choice,
But to succumb to the rules and laws,
Of the divine, yet something happened,
Uncalled for, much ghastly to witness even...

Continued...

The Bride (Part Three)

'The Bride', once her cascading arrival,
Into his hollow abode, where never glee,
Laughed neither there were hues of love,
Turned the most mightiest, the cruellest,
Into a kind hearted 'God', where then,
His reign made of darkest, blackest clouds,

Changed into white, like milk incessantly,
Flowing from the heavens, where no bird,
Dared sore till the highs and chirped on,
Their threshold and golden boughs, waking,
Them up to the beautiful dawns which he,
Had never witnessed earlier, his vastness,

Into a tiny warm shell, where the twain,
Souls dwelled, she had filled his hearth with,
Endless mirth, alas! Tonight that tenet got,
Broken, an earthly woman conjured by her,
Beloved husband, for once the hour glass,
Clogged, the sand holding the abysmal time,

Their unison, their sanctimonious love seeing,
A horrible end, the sound of those uncanny,
'Neighs' of carcass horses showing impatience,
And the chariot's holder, whipping time and,

Again its slash, came closer and held her,
Husband's hand, ripping his skin, took away,

His soul, the youngest God's corpse then fell,
On the floors of heaven, the bride who has,
Been a mute observer, for long when alive,
And long when she died, knew all the secrets,
Of doors seven and the one leading to hell,
Her soul roved in space, meeting the goddesses,

A noble and kind soul, she received myriad,
Blessings, she could turn any heart stone with,
Her furious eyes, her resentment began roaring,
Into the skies, lightning and thunderstorm,
Was seen again, the bride's red attire and she,
Were burning, she strode near and opened,

Her eyes, looking straight towards that devil's
Face, and soon his heart turned into stone,
She then snatched her husband's soul from,
The chasm of hell, and brought him to life,
The benign lord watching all, was touched,
By their deep love, blessed them eternity,

And love filled life; they lived in their kingdom,
With much glee, much joy as their bearing,
'The Bride' was an earthly woman, born with,
A womb to carry child, she gave him seven,
Who grew up listening to their parent's love tale!
Telling the world same, when they all emerged in the
sky...

End

The Cracked Tea Cup

Towards the inside room, I saw a tattered sofa,
Lying alongside the wall, a tea cup on the table,
With a prominent crack on body, it sat alone, visible,
It looked old or has been made old, there was dust,
Inside, it bore the marks of time, when it was regal,
As I watched the cup, myriad chapters unfolded,
It spoke to me of those times, once alive blissful times!

I saw all with my eyes closed and the films rolled,
The curtains were lifted; a stage of life came alive,
The actors' faces I couldn't see, they wore a veil,
Yet, they touched a strange chord of my heart, and it,
Rung and rung in my ears the music so familiar,
The melodies long lost some were in space,
The dialogues started coming out of my lips,

Like I was the character and it was my life play,
The proscenium stage of my life drama and I,
Changed myriad makeovers with time and tide,
As I was the puppet on the stage such wide,
And the strings attached with something that,
Made me dance, laugh, cry, love and romance,
Or! Perhaps by someone who made my gestures and
all!

Though never I saw the puppeteer, but he was always there,
And the play ended, I opened my eyes, saw the same cup,
Sitting on the same table cracked and covered in dust,
It has lost its shine, newness, but it still exists,
The play in which it was used no longer amazes,
The crowd of those many faces who came to watch,
The show, all is now dust and dead, curtains rise no more,

Only the mystic smell of oldness has spread all over,
The costumes once used by me are hanging in mute,
The colourful life drama is over, yet my heart holds many,
Stories which I want to enact, but still on that dead stage,
The puppeteer's laugh I hear, he still remains hidden,
And the strings are with him; so long they shall be,
The mightiest will make me move on his will, so be it!

And for the last time gazed I at the cracked tea cup,
The cracks were the mark of much history left behind,
But still making its way into the present, perhaps,
In future too it will leave its impression for those,
And I stole some time from the moment, saw my face,
On the cracks realizing I exist too in the present,
And it wasn't the story of the cracked tea cup at all,
It's of those faces, that reflects on the cup now and again...

The Day I Lived Again

Lying void on the carpet of green meadows,
Frozen, wrapping the sheet of death almost,
Eyes wide open and awake looking up in the sky,
The clouds passing hastily, like heaven's express,
Saw the Dandelions floating, slowly and freely,
The short lived ones, but didn't heard their complains,
Flying was I too, liberated, crossed the Dandelions
even,

Met on the way ahead, marvellous colourful winged,
Butterflies, flying wherever they wished, no chains,
And barriers to tie their feet, they had all the riches,
Autumn's sister came, the spring held my hand,
She took me to the bed of flowers, spread so vast,
Ran and ran I the whole time, carefree and joyful,
On my way then met, the bumble bees buzzing,

Buzzing around and around the prettiest blossoms,
What sight of romance! Blossoms hesitant from their,
Lovers' smiled and the buzzing grew louder and
louder,
The blossoms came to them bowing down the boughs,
Breaking the manacles, to unite with their lovers,
Feeling jealous of their love, yet I admired the beauty,
Spring showed me, still stuck in the fall hitherto,
Collecting, wrecked pieces of life falling on the ground,

Clinging so badly, unaware that spring will come,
She did come, and said to me, "What holds your feet,
fly high!
Look! My sister sacrifices herself, smiling with
gratitude,
For me to arrive, old clothes are shed in kindness,
New skin is worn, why cling to what bounds you,"
The spring taught me the lessons of life, perhaps death,
I must say, it took me by surprise they die, rise again,

Still so much pride in their eyes of living short,
Yet meaningful, joyous and precious life, which I saw,
Then she left my hand, the blossoms and bumble bees,
The bed of flowers and the butterflies, the Dandelions,
They all left me behind; moving fro, I was left behind!
Again seeing the clouds express, with eyes wide awake,
Feeling the cool breeze against my skin, I realized,
I died long before, or perhaps it was the day I lived
again...

The Duvet Dream

Lost in the stillness of dark hours,
I stepped into another world, calm,
And peaceful it should be, wearing red,
Like a bride, I am someplace unknown,
The faces too unknown around me,
I sense a different person I am, looking,
Different with another woman face,
Yet my soul same keeps probing,
For those known faces, whom I have known,
Who are mine, amid that bizarre crowd!
I am lost; my individuality lost, yet my soul,
Same keeps looking for them, again and again,
I am wandering, running to find them,
That faces who have stayed with me,
Who were part of me, yet I have forgotten!
My eyes are looking for a man, my lover,
Only him I remember, his face so vivid,
He is somewhere; I know he is there,
I do not like this new stranger in my life,
His face not seen, yet I know he is there too,
Somebody forcing me into this alien,
Relationship I don't want to step in,
My heart is longing for my lover,
I want to go to him, into his warm embrace,
Which I have felt around me,
Why I am not able to find him, my soul,

Is making me suffer this parting,
Of twain bodies, of that love, of romance,
My eyes are only searching for him,
Everywhere, he is the one I love!
Fearful I am perspiring beneath that red dress,
Suddenly I wake up under my duvet,
Real wet in sweat, my heart beating faster,
I know it's a dream and I am sitting awake,
Beside my lover, who is still in his slumber!
I was gasping then with a relieved sigh,
I realized he was near not gone far,
Yet the fear of losing him even in my dream,
Was more than a nightmare and it lingers,
Still inside me whenever I get inside the duvet...

The Ghost Woman

In a narrow tunnel, beneath the Mahal,
There were webs and centipede crawling,

A strange kind of stale air suffocating the,
Nostrils, and that eeriness which gave me,

Goosebumps and chills down my spine,
A teenager girl I was with curious mind,

The place attracted me then to explore,
I waited for the warm days to begin,

When we were free to roam around,
The whole reign of the haunted kings and,

Their hunting abode, a stone structure,
With only two floors, we went there,

And played in the daytime, and saw never,
Dead kings walking or ghosts but that,

Tunnel was where we always wanted to go,
But we dared not to, the whole place was,

Fearsome, still our young hearts never,
Cared, and one day we dared, entered the,

Tunnel and kept going, it was small one,
Me and my brother holding hands,

Walking leisurely, hearing beats own,
And when we reached the light, the end,

Of the tunnel we saw a beautiful woman,
Smiling at us, we were half dead and fell,

There was no thought; we knew she was that,
A ghost, a soul still haunting the Mahal,

Yet in the chaos I noticed she was beautiful,
A Nepalese woman, wearing traditional attire,

In that moment thought we, here how came,
A woman from hills and to our guts that has,

Gone lose, we ran to our hearts and never,
Gazed behind, she said no word and only smiled,

The incident scared us, stole our sleeps,
And disturbed and panicked we told at home,

My mother rescued us saying she was,
No ghost, the wife of a night guard she,

Had come to visit her husband, what sigh!
We were relieved, our young hearts delighted,

And we went again to the Mahal, played there,
Climbing to the roof, hiding behind the kaput,

Walls playing hide and seek, and time passed,
We grew adults, once again the Mahal stood,

In its solace, silent and eerie, there were no giggles,
No laughter of ours, perhaps the place missed us,

Even enjoyed or those invisible eyes, and never,
Came to scare us, but a news did, the Nepalese lady,

Was murdered with an axe, in her hometown,
Our hearts were sore, that day was our last,

Even to glance at the Mahal or talk about,
The tunnel was there, but the absence became more,

Frightening than her presence, we didn't wanted,
To see her sitting again at the end of the tunnel!

The Infinite Journey

When was I born and where was I born?
I have no past, no history; the door to ambiguity,
I opened my eyes in aloof, where no one watched,
No one knew when did I became this tender leaf,
The soft green colour gave me pride, I was young,
From the rest of them, they were matured more,
Still I wondered who I was, who am I!

There are so many and so many like me,
We all were young and I became friends,
We played with the wind and so did he played,
In return, every time I slept he shook me awake,
This kept going on and I grew young,
The breeze was same and it played with me same,
 *But, n*ow its touch on my body felt different,
The breeze came much quietly, shaking my chastity,

I didn't know when, I became aware of my body,
My youth at apex, blushed in the prettiest green,
I made others inferior and took too much pride,
The other leaves whispered to the breeze, of my conceit,
And one day, he came with all might and flew me
aside,
I was flying in love, ignorant me, innocent me,
Was flying with the breeze to where he flew,

Seeing dreams with closed eyes, of home and more,
Foolish I didn't realize the breeze has no one,
No home and nowhere to discontinue its journey,
The infinite journey of him, it fetched along it liked,
And left behind what didn't, and so I fell down,
He let me go, fall down into the vast calm rivulet,
This time I opened my eyes, and saw him for first,

My journey with him was over; I fell whirling, twirling,
It gave me the chance to fly high, to live his life,
I now sat on the river water; bit by bit it gulped me,
Into its realm of wetness, my tears mixed in vast,
Water becoming alike and from tender green,
I turned brown wet, and drowned deeper much deep,
He left me in aloofness or vastness, the journey has
begun,
Now I am dreaming with open eyes, my eyes sky
high…

The Lantern Night

Darkness outside, and the ghostly breeze,
I stood there alone shivering as it teased,
The raven sky, with no star that twinkled,
Even in the farthest, and my skin shrinked,
In fear, and the trees seemed uncanny,
With their boughs swishing with the gust,
Looking like hands trying to fetch my soul,

I tip toed not to wake the dryads of night,
I didn't wanted my soul to be taken, they,
Were all ogling at me, I was a prey, a woman!
You left me my beloved leaving no word,
I stood in the middle and couldn't go back,
My heart was sore, for I had left in our hearth,
Twain naive hearts, lost in their sweet slumber,

And that night seemed longer than others,
My eyes were wet, I had two precious,
One those were left behind, other I hadn't found,
Yet, I had to be back home before it was dawn,
Before the birds tweeted the morning melodies,
Into their ears, my son's would soon be awake,
Alas! I had to tread that path of dare and doom,

Aghast! My heart beats got smelled far,
At last fell the marauding eyes all over me,
And one step ahead I was to be eaten,
Ah! My beloved I couldn't, forgive me!
I couldn't cross that line, I knew you were,
Near but far to my eyes, I sensed in the air,
Twain eyes yours, watched me in the dark,

Reading my fear and timidity, I had but,
That one night to bring you back, with,
Sun's virgin light you shall be gone forever,
Knowing all I cried, I cried to heart's desire,
And holding up the lantern for once in dark,
I saw many ghostly faces, but not yours,
They had their mouths opened, lurking lust,

Man was the new ghost in town,
In your shadow had I been for long,
It was time for me to return, and did I,
Inside the hearth it was silent as it was,
When you left me crying on the facade,
My motherhood chained me to go no further,
With tears myriad, I quietly got under the duvet,

Of despair, clinging to the naive bodies of,
My innocent offspring's, trying to find solace,
With dawn you came, Ah! My beloved,
My mate, you came, I had tears and thy eyes wet,
And you embraced me into thine arms,
Whispering into my ears those words,
Only you, me and heaven knows,

The dawn arrived filling brightness into my hearth,
Yet I forbid that lantern night, the worst night ever!
But the oil filled lamp, did lit our dark space in silence...

That Mulberry Gust

Two curious eyes staring, from behind glass,
Panes of a window, which opened to a small,
Porch at the back, stood there in its silence,
A grown mulberry, the breeze made the berries,
Swing along to its tune, some fell on earth,
And brought a smile, on a little girl's face,

She never ate them, but enjoyed their fall,
And the bower so fine, keeping the small,
House at dead end, wrapped in its cold arms,
An isolated place in world, it was hearth,
It was home, for hours she played under,
The shade of mulberry, and at night the,

Same tree was eerie, with its black branches,
Touching the panes, making the knock with,
Every gust, and the leaves whispering the,
Lullabies of night, even the gamut of twinkles,
Watched the little girl, still awake with big eyes,
How the night passed away, and days many!

When, those days turned into years and more,
Oh! Much long time had gone by, yore!
Today standing in my galleria, melancholia,
I wore, my soul's attire, I found saffron hued,
Mulberry leaf along with a dried berry,

The breeze had brought along, and had,
Brought the emotions of the days bygone,

Lying in the corner of galleria, speaking,
Telling me, its story in myriad mute words,
I picked up the leaf, in one glance I was there,
Standing small in front of that big tree,
I saw that little girl again giggling, laughing,
I opened my eyes, tears resting on the sides,

Ah! She is still there, happy and blithe,
She still runs around inside and outside,
That small house, where even that tree,
Enjoys her company, and in mediocre here,
Left is all a nostalgic poetess, wandering,
In past lane, trying to find those lost moments,
That the mulberry gust had brought along...

The Sculptor's Sculpture

He loved his hands, they were his God,
The sculptor, played with mud his gold,
His hearth a mess, filled with clay and dust,
Shared with his wife, a lonely woman inside
Her pretty face gloomy and her heart cried,
The sculptor for days and nights made art,
His fingers danced on clay, not on body her's,
A pair of tearful eyes watched it all,
In silence, her heart kept clandestinely,
Beating for the sculptor, who remained lost in art!

And his lady behind the door of their nuptial,
Bond silently weeping bearing her life's fall,
His masculine body danced from here to there
With silent rhythms in the air, he swirled fair,
He dwindled there, rose and danced again,
To his sculpts that spoke of animal and birds,
His petite landscape were eye catchers,
He made it all with virgin clay, somewhere,
Forgot his virgin wife waits in dismay,
His finger touched none, and so was he done,

Satisfied in nature's lobby, touched no naked body,
No bosom, no heart, no tears, was in his share,
He had a mate, yet alone, aloof he fared,
One sunset his fingers ached, he sat down,

On his chair, in these many years, he gazed,
What beaming beauty his space savoured!
His young wife budding like lotus in still waters,
Blushed her cheeks like fresh lilies,
Her narrow long neck holding pearls in panache,
Her heart beats he heard for the first,

Thumping fast beneath her fair bosom,
He saw, yes! He saw a sculpted figurine,
Her heart's light entered his eyes,
Ah! What buxom beauty in his hive,
He roared his manhood, filled her in his arms,
He crushed her into his strength and charm
A handsome artist now played with his muse,
And for the first his hands danced abuse,
His fingers danced on God's sculpture,
Her naked body was his, she waited this,

Spring entered into their abode, stayed long,
Much long, the sculptor and his soul mate,
Lost in the arms of romance night till dawn,
And the dust! All clay remained untouched,
He embraced her, loved her, and kept her,
Safe in his chest, alas! He born to sculpt,
Only, couldn't stand destiny's clever game,
She was there for moments, to earn him fame,
On the decided day of fall, she was laid on,
Her death bed and asked for a favour,

Do not bury me, do not burn, do not fetch,
My body to the forlorn! Sculpt me, sculpt me!
Oh! My poor husband, make me your piece of art,

And shall I then remain forever in your heart,
The sculptor cried and cried and his tears,
Was the water he kneaded the clay dough with,
On her earthly body he put lumps and lumps,
Of clay, dead long ago she felt no pain,
Neither a tinge of cold on her fair skin,
Dawn till dark, his hands worked hard,

He fell upon earth's chest, his sculpture done,
Lying flat with emotions weighing him down,
And with virgin ray of sun, she shined in grim,
Her loving soul was still alive, caged forever,
Inside and she seemed the most petite,
The mud showed all, her curves and her fall,
She stood in front of him, his wife a mud doll,
Of flesh and blood, he embraced her for last,
And gave her away to the world, his first,
Human sculpture ah! She taught him real art,

The Sculptor's name spread in the air, praising,
Came for his lady love, and he roamed around,
And around to myriad corners of the ball,
He was a man and yes! He was, found love again,
In dark eyes of a lady, she stood tall in pride,
The sculptor's prosperity she gained, she tamed,
It was no love at all and soon came again the fall,
The day his first wife was made clay,
He was breathing, just living in her memories,
Barely living, her sacrifice was much greater than his,

Fame, alas! In aloofness and slumber his clay wife,
Is forgotten now, she rests in dark museum,

A piece of art now she is; no one sees her love,
No one cares the tale, yet they saw the real tears,
That still flows down her stoned cheeks,
She is named lady of tears, and that's all,
The sculptor's sculpture no one knew was,
A real woman, who loved her husband much,
She gave him the gift of her flesh and blood,
And now she stands only a breathless mud doll,

Perchance! For eyes myriad and still comes the fall!
For her lover and their love, yes still comes the fall!

The Shrine She Lives Through

The fresh morning dew, on the flowers and grass,
She woke with dawn's virgin ray falling on Sitar,
Praying and paying homage at first, she touched,
The sacred Sitar, her thin fingers danced on the wires,
Bursting the morning with its divine music, along her
voice,
Her morning raga enchanting, echoing and chaste,
Flowed her lyrical tunes across and vast travelled they,

Sitting on the chariot of breezes, they took her voice,
Far and farther with each new day, and so does she,
Travelled in her mind and soul, to the shrines of love,
And those temples of ecstasy of Lord, two souls
entwined,
Postures of sensual love, fiery passion blazed into the
sun,
He touched her from the soul, and her voice became
deep,
Her raga was touched again and again till she perspired,

Beneath her white cloth, droplets of sweat made her
wet,
Bare body chaste for them, but secretly touched by
Lord,

She felt his hands moving on her; top to bottom she shivered,
Suddenly growing ecstatically insane, in love pure for her Lord,
Taking her out of this world, she needed no man's feel,
Neither company of God's sons, to break her preserved chastity,

She lived and experienced more than as a human,
Her love so pious, and untouched, she awoke the Lord,
From his shrine each dawn, and he did came in soul,
Drawn towards her divine music, and towards her earthly body,
They merged, embraced in space, only the universe knew,
This story of woman and God's tabooed love, goddess's in awe,
Felt envious often, ah! What tale of immodest pious love,

Before the rays touched the virgin earth and birds woke,
Their unison was over, myriad people came to worship,
Their lord in the temple, with garlands and incense sticks,
The deity stood soulless though, embraced in erotic love,
Ah! What power her music had, lord came into her abode,
She was a chaste in her human avatar, though not to Lord,

Her sitar played each day and morning, fingers danced magic,

What blissful love was, invisible for the world to see, be known,

The Sitar now covered with dust and morning dew still,

Sits on the flowers and grass, the Lord's deity is standing,

Till now worshiped by many, still are they clandestine lovers,

She sings for her lover, heard only by him, soundless music in world,

They still make love unseen before, and ever, as man and woman,

Folks say and believe, she lives through the shrine; a pure devout,

She the pious devout of her time, with great respect now her Sitar

Rests beside the Lord, she is his forever, a benign soul in his shrine...

Glossary

Sitar a large, long-necked Indian lute with movable frets, played with a wire pick.

The Stairs

Time shall cometh one day know I,
When this attire of flesh would,
Worn out, and my arms around thy,
Body shall then embrace you much tight,
I'll not let you go, and show my fight,
Amid twain worlds of flesh and soul,
I'll con it to the fire, and to the dust,

You never rose from dust, know why?
The keepers of heaven are begging,
To take thy flesh and make it soil,
You never born from ashes, know when?
The grievers would come, and set ablaze,
Turning you that gray dust, my eyes despise,
My arms are still around thy body,

My tears not dry yet, the salt is white,
On my cheeks and time is shallow,
It would one day compel me to give up,
But this moment, I was firm and didn't let,
Thy body leave that facade, where I gazed,
Myriad shadows trying to heave us apart,
Our earthly love was over, but soul love,

Yet has to begun, Alas! I am an elfin,
In front of fate's gullible game, hath I,

Ever knew the breeze of dismay would come,
So hushed without ever knocking, it stole,
My beloved's breath, yet my clasp to his,
Hand was rigid not letting go, I saw through,
My watery eyes, thy soul climbing the stairs,

One glance you gazed at me behind,
And my heart skipped myriad beats,
That day, now in this transient world,
I am waiting for the stairs to arrive,
Yet again, to see you for once when you,
Shall arrive and take my hand, I'll be all,
Yours forever then, much I miss thine embrace...

Timeless Frozen Love of an Epoch

In the dark hours of night, she kept waiting for,
Her love to come back, but couldn't wait anymore,
Ran down the *stairs*, took the buggy standing outside,
Her heart was skipping many beats, worried she,
Perspired beneath her long flowing *gown*,
She knew, he was a *womanizer*, still loved him,

Her forgiveness he thought to be her innocence,
He faked loving her, knew she all still loved him more,
Poor he! Couldn't understand and she never forced him,
He lived a rich man's life, with many women around,
He threw money and time, staying not for long,
With one woman, it was his regal addiction,
Wine and women, yes! He was a womanizer!

Tonight was special; it was their centennial night,
She wore a fine dress, sitting beside the candle light,
She spent till midnight gazing at the staircase,
Ears alert to hear his footsteps, in that chilling night,
Never did she heard the footsteps, and ever the clock stopped,
The house was full with the sound of 'tick tock',

Half past midnight and she couldn't wait more,
She wore no shawl, running through the vestibule,
Running down the stairs, she looked hurt and in pain,
Her beautiful white gown following her, was stained
mud,
Alas! She came to the brothel, sure of where to find
him,
He was shocked to see his wife, standing in front of
him,

Not a single word, she uttered, went back the same
way,
She came from; he didn't have the courage to face her,
He never followed her home, made an unpardonable
mistake,
She kept looking back from her buggy; tears froze near
the eyes,
Not even heavens knew what she had in mind,
Silently she arrived to their loving abode,
Stood in the gallery, that opened outside,

Standing for a while, she felt the chill against her skin,
Shedding off all her clothes, she sat naked whole night,
Slowly embracing the ice on her bare body, she froze,
The maids were done for the day, no one was there,
To save their mistress, she didn't wanted to be saved
either,
In imperial lights of the city, she got lost in frosty
darkness,

And so her pure love froze, she turned into a blue
beauty,

Blood in her veins became ice, night passed away,
With the virgin ray of dawn, he arrived,
It was late for eternity, his shrieks the city heard,
He looked at her blue face; she was still beautiful,
They say! He kept her body in a glass coffin till,
His last breath, yes! He made penances for eternity,

Alas! He was a womanizer, from then on their love,
Became a timeless chronicle, of a frozen epoch,
With the first snowflake, they say a beautiful,
Woman is seldom, still seen running across the streets,
Holding her gown, she always seems in haste,
Merging into the white snow, she disappears,
Many have seen except him, it was the reprimand,
Oh poor him! He paid the price for being a womanizer...

Unfaithful Love

The first beam of sun knocked,
Her eyelids and arouse she,
From her slumber of yore years,
Gazing at her beloved's face,
She blushed and embraced,
Putting her silken robe, tiding,
The tresses tangled from nights',
Romance her bare body beneath,
Still lingering fresh with odour,
Of their love tale, her face yet pale,

She took one glance, her reflection,
On the mirror, she was beautiful,
Her swollen eyes of ten years siesta,
Gave her the hint, it was time ripe,
She was awakened to face the tempest,
That kept coming and sullying,
Her fragile house, breaking apart,
The liaisons tied of invisible thread,
And the heaven's roared and roared,
To make her awake of the deep trance,

She never heard, busy weaving dreams,
And they saw how her young heart,
Was in glee, playing with sand and,
Making a dwelling alongside the shore,

It was time she woke, and so they broke,
Her castle, the sand got washed away,
And she stood cold wet in her own tears,
In a little while they pushed, she fell down,
It was the biggest jolt she could bear,
Her eyes opened wide to that virgin dawn,

And she found her unclothed body,
Lying alongside her beloved's,
In long time she experienced bodily love,
She had been long in her wakeful slumber,
Walking, talking, breathing and lamenting,
Nightmarish defiant dreams were over,
And for first she put kohl in her eyes,
Opened the doors to the galleria,
And saw a squall approaching,
Gazing hard she made it turn its way,

Tis, her awakening to the unfaithful love,
Tis, her mourning to the unfaithful lust...

Where I Left My Shadow

Often the breeze blows strong, unknowingly,
Entering through the windows without knocking ever,
Turning the pages unturned for long, it rests there,
In the silence of my heart, still treasured as mine,
The love letters and more, those glory days of ours',
Safe in the most clandestine place on earth,

The zephyr the flirtiest, and the mightiest,
Seeks never permission, today it stirred again,
The melodies of lost time, sitting in my galleria,
Gazing at the blue sky, I am much bewildered,
The nights and day are just passing by,
Eyes are still waiting, more than I,

To see once and again, that one face on the mirror,
Reflecting, where I stood once and you gazed,
We talked in silence thousand words of love,
Beckoning to what our hearts desired, you touched,
My soul, the essence of your love is still lingering,
Within me, in my soul, I imbibed into you,

Hollowness and void this place seems on surface,
And deep within, leaving was an easy way out,
Still for hours I look at the mirror to get a glance of,
That known face or that stranger's image perhaps,

I am here so caught and wrecked, sharing this space,
I desired to with you, only a male body now surrounds
me,

My fight with time has shaped into a mêlée,
Two bodies draped into the garment of thorns,
Bruising, tearing cutting each other's flesh,
A mute victim in the house of God, I ask oft,
Perhaps, the answers are much silent or my prayers,
She is not the woman anymore in the mirror,

I am, she had long gone along leaving me behind,
The doors are locked and jammed, I tried hard,
To escape this rape, from vicious web of life,
Envious me, I scourged her who left me and this
Abyss along with you, now I am just a body without
soul,
Wandering often! Places, where I left my shadow...

Whispering Murmurs

Last night I heard the night whisper,
To the moon, "Darling aren't you in glee,
You shall be in my arms for long now,
And we shall make love for eternity",
She then silently whispered into the,
Ears of her sole lover, "My dearest I am"
The night smiled and filling her into,
His embrace he asked, "Tell me aren't,
You feeling richer now, for the day who,
Was evermore thy foe, shall soon sink,
Into the abyss of horizon, no longer it,
Shall be able to keep us far, oh! My sweet,
Beloved our glory days shall reach far,"
And again I heard her whisper calmly,
While kissing gently on night's brawny,
Cheeks, "Yes my dearest lover, I do",
And I saw the night's chest swelling in,
Pride, he then held her tighter as she,
Sighed, her cheeks blushing more greyer,
The night then said with a frown, "promise,
Me my sweetheart, that thy love stays same,
Even when its summer and winter's game,
The rain is the most callous, it hides you in,
His darkest veil, those are my murky days,
When I can't glance, thy iridescent body,
Thus my love, my head remains ever,

Bowed to the autumn, he is the kindest,
Mate, yes! My beloved I hear the autumn's,
Footsteps round the corner, I am eager aren't you",
The moon shyly hid her face into night's embrace,
And replied in the most innocent voice, "Yes, my,
Love I am", soon she got merged into the darkest,
Veil of night, twain lovers got lost into another,
Realm of making love, silence prevailing all over,
As far my eyes could see, I only saw the most,
Ravenous night, I then left the lovers in,
Their solace, getting inside the duvet I thanked,
Them, for telling the news, I loved autumn,
Just like them, the season of shedding and,
Standing a bare soul, yet being most beautiful,
An uncanny autumn zephyr then murmured into,
My ears playing with my tresses, soon then I,
Too sank into the embrace of my earthly lover...

Musings of the Poetess

~ 1 ~

He had a chest deep and vast,
Where he hid all his thoughts,
Never letting anyone inside,
He sailed alone, on high tides,
Of kaput emotions, and when,
The waves of ocean were low,
Malleable he took his muse,
Along and sank beneath in glee,
Allowing her to read his mind,
And in those times they made love!

~ 2 ~

Sometimes in my wakefulness,
I see views of a life that still,
Doesn't belongs to me, and,
My iffy mind consoles the heart!
It's thy soul's window that has,
Opened to a new horizon, for now,
Its wetting your senses with a,
Handful of a twinkling future's cascade!

~ 3 ~

I thought thy love was sane,
It was all sense and logic,
Commingled with a twinge,
That you threw more oft!
At my half wounded heart,
But you tore apart the heaven,
When they took me from you,
That day I saw, thine insane love!

~ 4 ~

Tonight the moon came to my galleria,
And whispered the clandestine words,
Die more to win his love, like do I,
With every dawn, and my beloved,
Awaits to see my soul blooming,
The brightest on full moon nights...

~ 5 ~

I was in slumber when the squall,
Arrived, and when I rose all I saw,
Was a wretched house and stood,
There alone, sank in my own tears,
But this time I remained awake,
Too see how horrid could it be,
And to my heart's courage it couldn't
Meet my eyes and altered its way!

~ 6 ~

There was something about his eyes,
That watched her whilst she was lost in,
Her own mundane world, and when near,
His love was ever rigid, he never gazed,
Her pretty face, she knew his adamant,
Love, but never uttered a word, though,
Blushed in her solitude with her cheeks,
Pink like a fresh lotus bud, she was his queen!

~ 7 ~

He had a clandestine pocket where he hid,
His muse's pretty face, painted by his heart,
Never revealing to her, only defiance,
And odious love, mute words of abuse,
Were his gestures towards her, and day!
One the portrait fell down from his keep,
He thought saw none, caressing he hid,
It same place, she knew now he,
Loved her only his love was,
Clandestine like his concise...

~ 8 ~

He loved his chemise white and crisp,
Not a stain should ever be missed,
He hung white one after another,
Chemise were myriad attached to hangers,

Ah! She loved colours, and this he loathed,
No other hues were added or endorsed,
Ever to be kept in the closet and,
Even in their nest, the white deviant,
Love of ever his, became a curse when,
She was laid on the white! Breathless,
That day white became his irk, yet,
Alas! He was ever so late to even hate...

~ 9 ~

She was standing sinuous, a culprit,
Suppressing impish thoughts in her chest,
She has fallen for another man, alas!
But she knew she could bury her heart,
Along with her grave, never letting know,
Anyone, but not in god's house she would,
Be pardoned, what will she answer them?
Infidelity was it a crime! Certainly love was not...

~ 10 ~

I could see the horizon,
Standing in my galleria,
I saw the flocks of birds,
Returning to their nests,
With mist they explore,
The sky, with dusk they,
Refuge into their small hearth,
My soul's voyage is similar,

As far it flies, by the end,
It longs for that home,
Those four walls,
From where it began all!

~ 11 ~

I am leaving my tears as trails
For you to follow, when you wake up,
From your deep slumber of pride,
And find the pillows wet, soon you will,
Realize they were yours from night,
Not mine, only the dried salt from my tears,
Would lead you to where I had gone long...

~ 12 ~

Lovers from birth after birth,
Our souls have chosen this body,
And before its dust let's not ravage,
The time precious, let's make again love..

~ 13 ~

This summer she was in plain cotton,
Perspiring beneath clothes, with sighs,
Many and myriad grins, she gave to him,
In these hot days and nights, much like,
Pearls they sat on her dusky skin, those,

Droplets of sweat that oft dripped from,
Her face fine, flowing like a rivulet till her,
Bosoms and got lost somewhere in the heart,
Her's, the blouse all wet, and solely knows he,
How much wait for summer he does year every...

~ 14 ~

He said, spread you wings and soar high,
Though never revealed had a dagger hidden inside,
A casket, yet she could breathe that corroded
iron smell,
And so she veiled her wings beneath,
her skin that often fluttered, reminding all the time,
of her clandestine defiant dreams!

~ 15 ~

I am not only leaving my words,
Written in black on the blank pages,
It's my heart resting in every word,
And if you ever shall pick those letters,
They'll become water in your cupped palms,
From the myriad tears I had hidden as verse...

~ 16 ~

She kept the earthen lamp on the facade,
Filled with oil, so it remained awake,

Till the dark hours to give light to the lost,
Ones and those who left behind their hives,
And all blessed her for whoever passed,
That darkest lane where her hearth stood,
Alas! She lived in a brothel, yet her soul was pious...

~ 17 ~

Million words of mayhem melt,
My soul in dismay, but one word of thy love,
Gives me refuge and I melt in thine embrace!

~ 18 ~

In the beginning there were myriad tears,
That shaped an ocean, and in the same ocean,
I found you waiting deep down beneath,
With a golden heart, and I decided to drown...

~ 19 ~

A decade passed for him to utter words,
Of keeping her as his muse,
And a century more he remained salacious,
Towards her earthly body,
Alas! But eternity to articulate his true love,
And now what use of shedding,
Tears few over her sepulchre!

~ 20 ~

The creased skin and hair grey,
One day shall be gone they,
And had I cried last night!
Tells the truth my swollen eyes,
Tis, a pang my heart shall hold,
Ever my breaths are still,
And how hard I desire, if I could,
For once,
And forever clog the time!

~ 21 ~

Perhaps! He never heard them before,
Even didn't cared it rested there,
But the day, when he found her,
For first then he heard his heart beats,
And it felt, like for so long he has,
Been dead, now has he come alive solely for her!

~ 22 ~

It seemed she was probing something,
Hitherto she looked, into the derelict,
Standing dwellings many, through the,
Fissures and broken casements, passing,
Through doors ajar now and then,
Where was that wooden chest? She thought,
It rests there her skeleton that was kept,

Long ago, she was still looking for it,
Her face seemed worried, yet had an incessant glow

~ 23 ~

Thy hands joined together, eyes upon,
The sky, thy lips moving soft with,
Inaudible words myriad, only I heard,
The sounds of sigh! I asked seldom times,
Hath you been praying? For my well being,
Frequent uh-uh he answered, moving his,
Skull from left to right, how naive is?
Lover mine, doesn't even know to lie...

~ 24 ~

How it all begun? How the days,
Turned to months, and months to,
Years many, and soon decades passed,
Twain earthly souls began their,
Love story from a bed, yet again,
They are laying old aged, with skin,
Creased to folds many, once there were,
Battles of sleep on that bed!
And those who fought have flown,
Away, now they sleep with much,
Space, isn't this they had wished?
Throughout those times, alas!
For a body now that has shrinked,
The same bed now seems immense...

~ 25 ~

What was fear? What was love?
I had known fear, of being dead,
Someday and not found by many,
But the moment I tasted love,
Fear became more prominent,
It didn't leave me, rather embraced,
Me tighter, then I knew love,
Was the fear, making me weak...

~ 26 ~

I escaped seven heavens,
I fled athwart into six skies,
I merged five elements,
Within me and four corners,
I left behind, I dwelled,
In births three before I,
Met thou, then leaving twain,
Doors ajar never turned,
Behind, I have come for you,
The one man you!
And thy sole love!

~ 27 ~

It was the ether of his soul,
That travelled miles across,
She smelt too his essence,

In her unsound slumber,
With dreams wet as she rolled,
Throughout night over the bed,
Sensing the mannish warmth,
By her side, on her bare skin,
That he sent her along with,
His incessantly flowing musk breaths!

~ 28 ~

The fall has come, awaken!
But don't make sounds loud,
I know the zephyr swishes,
The boughs and oh see! Fell,
Down another saffron leave,
Hush still, we don't raise our,
Moaning, they are not for others,
To hear, those marauding eyes,
Will ogle thine earthly love, let him,
Know alone this fall and,
More many yet to come,
Your bare body is merely,
For him, let him savour thy soul,
And make love, even he wills eternity!

~ 29 ~

He was her God, she bathed him,
In pious love, her uncovered body she,
Surrendered into his feet, and her heart,

Was the shrine, dwelled he as a deity!
Offering every virgin morsel to him first,
She didn't fear the wrath of God's unseen...

~ 30 ~

I can merely give you, the gift of poetry,
The black words on the white are my,
Soul's voice, if they ever reach your,
Threshold than I shall be freed from the,
Burden of regret that I had never said,
To you "I love you"!

~ 31 ~

The heaven cried too that day!
With heavy downpour was lightened,
Their heart, but his tears were incessant,
And fell myriad on breathless body her's,
He kissed her lips as many times,
To feel that touch, that warmth of,
Her, which had now turned into frost,
Alas! The famished flames gulped her all,
And he remained a meagre spectator,
Much of a mute beggar in God's house...

~ 32 ~

Read my bare soul overflowing,
With poetry, before its' late,

As eternity, ah! I am knocking,
Yet on every heart's door holding,
A bowl empty and still I am not,
Visible to thine eyes, but day one,
That mist from above the sky,
Shall carry me on its chariot,
To the farthest lands, perchance then,
Thy hands will hold the rotten pages,
Lying somewhere as dirt, spilling my verses,
Alas! Only that thud on thy doors with,
Fingers once those were fragile and bled,
Shall not disturb thy worldly sleep!

~ 33 ~

His touch was sedative, lulled her,
Into the realm of fantasy, and yet,
Why? She couldn't meet her own,
Eyes into the glass reflecting her,
Fair face, she now wished death,
More for him, and for her own body,
She was sinuous and so was he!

~ 34 ~

The night passed away,
Without a blink, I didn't wanted,
To miss any of the seconds running,
Incessantly of the timepiece, and,
The glimpse of thy face, yet before,

It was dawn, I had to close my,
Eyes, and shouldn't I tell you I had,
Never felt my body so cold, but the,
Drops of those warm salted water from,
Your eyes, on my face I still felt!

~ 35 ~

Yes! I am complete to go there,
Yes! I have taken the entire twinge,
As human, and now in my last hours,
I shall die with open eyes,
For they wish to see the tears,
In thine eyes, and did you loved me!
Else my soul wouldn't be satiated,
Submerging into the divine Ganges
And I must tell you that moment,
I shall turn into a Goddess!

~ 36 ~

Thy hatred is a burden to embrace,
Twinges my heart evermore,
Hath you whispered the words?
Of loathe to the universe, even to the skies,
They all turned my enemies,
The moment you stopped loving me!

~ 37 ~

I still have that muslin cloth,
Which you wrapped around,
My earthly body, filled with the,
Aroma of tuber roses from our,
Nuptial's night, that fragrance is,
Alive in my senses!
Alive in my soul!

~ 38 ~

You were on foot with an unhurried,
Pace carrying me in your brawny arms,
With my head resting against your chest,
And I smelt that essence of your musk
Elixir strongly into my nostrils and touch,
Of your masculine body as my tresses,
Swayed with your rhythmic moves and I felt
With closed eyes you gazed at my peaceful face,
And that moment I knew you could have made,
Love to me only if I wouldn't have died that day...

~ 39 ~

Even under the grave my earthly body,
Shall be yours and even when I turn,

All bones my astral soul shall be yours',
And if you find some dust into thine eyes,
That would bring tears, it shall be me,
Again making you cry if not in my,
Remembrance but merely for my ongoing,
Presence around you and in that void space,
Where I would be waiting evermore for thee...

~ 40 ~

Mayhems melt when tears flow from,
Lover's eyes, words appears noiseless,
When love becomes their language and,
Time seems frozen then, even for a moment...

~ 41 ~

Even the Gods made love amorously,
Yes! Even the Gods were sinful in their,
Deeds, they had the most marauding eyes,
Over the goddess's whom they created,
For their pleasure, and man his manifestation,
Now walks upon earth with same deeds,
Is more sinner than him! Is more amorous,
In loving a woman or lusting a woman,
This had always been there game,
Now why does he condemn sitting beyond?

~ 42 ~

My heart despised, yet my soul loved,
My lips uttered odious words, yet feared,
I and prayed not those to turn true,
My eyes irked your sight, yet longed,
To see when you were gone for long,
I searched escape, yet my feet jammed,
With your one caressing touch, and,
When abhorrence got tender I didn't,
Realize, yes! Truthfully it's solely you and,
Yours' making love that lingers within me!

~ 43 ~

Her tears fell on the floor and turned,
White pearls from the salt of her sobs,
She picked each pearls caressingly,
And tied them into string, making,
A garland of them, and the world,
Thought she was rich, yes! She was,
With the long waits she did for him,
Every night that gave her those pearls!

~ 44 ~

There were times when your love,
Appeared like sea, upon which I,

Shoved with ample water around me,
Yet I remained thirsty evermore!

~ 45 ~

Her earthly body was the source,
Of his bodily love, he was blissful,
To see her evermore uncovered,
Teasing her yet being aroused oft more,
Making love as ever he desired,
And the night she took her last,
Breath her corporeal body was no,
Longer he could keep, alas! His,
Eyes opened to a bitter truth...

~ 46 ~

The darkness didn't frightened her anymore,
He made love to her in those darkest hours,
And she was blind in his sane love, needed,
No eyes to see their bodily love, she felt it,
On her bare skin and inside her soul more!

~ 47 ~

For lovers there are no precincts,
Neither night can steal their love,
Nor days myriad, time can merely,
Steal away their skin, their age,
Their body but not their souls,

They shall make love evermore,
In youthful heaven's attires!

~ 48 ~

Was the rain the saint or the sinner?
That day, it brought us much closer,
Under one roof after years of distance,
That we live each day as soul mates!

~ 49 ~

Why the journey is such?
With one breath it will be,
Over and I shall be disowned,
As if I never belonged...

~ 50 ~

Often lost, often found,
My soul plummets in a,
Rivulet of varied emotions,
Yet I realized there was one,
Hand that held me evermore...

~ 51 ~

I chose you long before my birth,
And you chose me, before yours,

Our souls have met before on an,
Another plane, loved and kissed,
Each other, yet the first meeting,
Here had again all that novel charm!

~ 52 ~

The cup of her heart was spilling love,
And it kept flowing till far, tasted by one,
Who filled his empty cup and stayed!

~ 53 ~

The dark hours whispered magic,
In my ears and my soul soon left,
Me in slumber, roving unseen realms,
And with dawn it came with handful,
Of tales which it eared from doors,
Myriad and the sigh of hearts whom,
It befriended with on its way,
Now I know why all the heroines,
Of my prose are much known to me!

~ 54 ~

I was standing alone on the world's stage,
The impish sprite laughed from behind,
Mocking more often, I had no horde to hear,
My voice, but I had my lord listening,
And he was the whole mob needed I!

~ 55 ~

I want to be known as your sane,
Beloved, I want to be known as,
Your prosaic spouse, you don't
Read my words, but you have,
Read my soul from where,
My poetry flows!

~ 56 ~

A girl was lost long back during her,
Childhood days and a woman was born,
A daughter sacrificed her hearth, her mirth,
A bride was prepared in red, when the bride,
Cried in unbearable pain, a mother was born,
When she left, nothing was remembered of,
Her past, her journey from a girl to a woman!
That woman who once stepped the threshold,
As a bride, now lays there merely her remnants!

~ 57 ~

I have merged well in the hue of your love,
And wear thy name as ornament of pride,
Yet my domicile is someplace else, my soul,
Has another dwelling, find me there if,
I am ever mislaid and you care to find...

~ 58 ~

I see you when you are not there,
I hear your voice when you are not,
Speaking, I feel your shadow when,
You are not around, am I becoming,
Insane in thy love, or is it my sanity,
Curing me towards insanity, of thy love!

~ 59 ~

I will reach their first and make,
The dwelling same, just like I did,
While on earth, waiting for you,
To come and you shall be never,
Lost, leaving one home beneath,
Finding same again above the sky!

~ 60 ~

Am I lost without you, I fear,
You have made me cling more,
To your possessive love and what,
Is that magic that pulls me at you?
The more I am far; I want to be near...

~ 61 ~

The twilight staying long on my porch,
And the night seeming far to the eyes,

The droplets of sweat resting on my,
Temple made him aware summer was,
Near! Even the hushed murmurs of,
It on the parched earth could not,
Hide it from him, when the gust burnt,
His skin, he kept me safe in his refuge!

~ 62 ~

Time is boundless,
Love is limitless,
Time comes to end,
With the end of lovers,
But love goes beyond,
Lovers meet again,
On another plane,
Love never dies,
It merely,
Kills the time!

~ 63 ~

Man doesn't cry, but when the world,
Sleeps in peace, he becomes the lover,
And cries in agony for his dear beloved,
Staring at the night, seeming much long...

~ 64 ~

Hatred is much small to survive,
In the heart of the lovers, it comes,

As fall and once the dried emotions,
Shed off, what remains is chaste love!

~ 65 ~

They shared the roof,
They shared the supper,
They shared the bodies,
And when the end came!
Half got merged into his,
Half got merged into her,
They were never detached,
They fooled even the heavens...

~ 66 ~

Her beauty was not to be contained,
In a vessel, she had none that could,
Please his eyes, but she gave him love,
That was enough for him till his last!

~ 67 ~

The clouds of despair showered rain,
Bringing emotions of past, those drops,
Were not from heaven, but from your,
Eyes, when you cried in solace in far,
There was rain over me and my roof!

~ 68 ~

I am hidden beneath the words,
My story is untold yet, my poem,
Is not written yet, my emotions,
Are lying in silence, between those,
Pages and black ink! That aren't,
Turned yet, but I am right there,
Breathing and waiting to be told...

~ 69 ~

Words were not needed to them,
Eyes spoke it all, and the feelings,
Were heard by both, yes! Once a man,
And once a woman does fall in love!

~ 70 ~

Did I belong there?
Was it my own?
I was taught not to call it my own,
Ever and so I did,
I left with a smile,
Came to which they taught me to,
Be mine till end,
Yet I wonder,
Why it seemed much like a tavern,
And not the place,
I could call home!

~ 71 ~

I have been to a realm,
Where time stopped for once,
The youth was caught,
And the moments,
Were caged, the faces,
Never grew old, I shall stay,
There as well forever...

~ 72 ~

A rich beggar with riches,
A Romeo with loveless heart,
Come to know love from a woman!

~ 73 ~

That elixir she knew was of her lover,
How strange! She didn't smelt it,
When he was around, but when far,
She smelt it everywhere around her...

~ 74 ~

Come let's fall in love,
One more time,
Let's be strangers,
To each other,

One more time!
Let's undo the present,
And be lovers again...

~ 75 ~

You held me tight that night in thy arms,
And kept me close long to thy warmth
But I was too late to feel all those,
My breath had followed the gust outside...

~ 76 ~

Forgive me if I am born with emotions,
I too last night asked my creator,
Why have you given me those when they,
Aren't supposed to come out in the front!

~ 77 ~

My darling! My beloved,
I see you in my dreams,
I know how much you love me!
Even my soul allows,
You to come there and,
Make love to me,
Or is it your soul that,
Is still a Romeo?
Probing and following,
The places your muse roams!

~ 78 ~

She was the queen of his heart,
She was the slave of his love,
She chose being both by will,
His love was possessive,
But it was merely for her!

~ 79 ~

The silence of thy words don't murder me,
Anymore, but your silent face kills me every time!
The roar of thy mighty voice don't scare me,
Anymore, but the roar of your soul still scares me!
The mayhem tells me, you are around evermore,
Merely I know how much safe I feel in thy refuge...

~ 80 ~

Is it the heart or the soul?
That is in pain,
The heart is able to forgive,
But the soul still bleeds,
In quieten when the,
Wounds on the heart,
Are callously touched!

~ 81 ~

The sanctuary was nowhere but,
Into her love, where he found,
Peace after roving myriad corners,
He became the pilgrim in his own,
Nest, where his muse lived!

~ 82 ~

I am fading away,
Slowly but gradually,
My identity once as,
A daughter is turning,
Into mist and one day,
I shall remain merely,
A stranger!
On that threshold!

~ 83 ~

Once I was gibberish,
Now a blistering diamond,
I made my worth felt,
I am nothing, but a woman!

~ 84 ~

Her hero is stone hearted,
He feels less, speaks less,
But learnt love, for his muse,
Is like rivulet who inked,
Marks of her abiding love,
By flowing incessantly,
Over his stone heart!

~ 85 ~

Why is it too heavy?
To carry the ashes,
When alive her love,
Remained a burden,
Now she is merely,
A handful of dust!

~ 86 ~

Who said, I had dipped in those waters,
That contains youth, my skin will crease,
As much as yours and eyes will be weary,
Before you know, I will see you and,
You shall see me growing old, time,
Is not on our side, not again in this birth!

~ 87 ~

He shed tears along,
When she cried,
Not from the eyes,
But from his heart!
Such was his love...

~ 88 ~

A Writer bleeds many times,
A poet dies and lives again,
On the white papers,
And my life is dangling between,
Both bleeding more and dying!

~ 89 ~

There was merely one door,
That kept them apart,
For longer, within two realms,
One was the outer world for him,
And the inside one for her,
At last! By end of those hours,
He knocked, his ears keen,
To hear her footsteps on,
The other side of that door,
That told him her presence...

~ 90 ~

I am the dreamer,
I am making a world,
For me, where words,
Shall be my wall,
The food on the table,
And clothes on my skin,
No, I am not a conformist,
I am the poet behind the walls!

~ 91 ~

The ceramic cups and saucers are often,
Stained, with the colour of melancholy,
When the red lipstick, leaves a mark on,
The edges of the fine bone china cup,
Its heart gets melted, by being touched,
With the most silent lips in the world!

~ 92 ~

She said softly in a whisper,
"Goodbye", and he never,
Answered, he didn't ever,
Wanted to let her go, so he,
Stopped the word from,
Coming out of his mouth!

~ 93 ~

My prayers begins with you,
And ends with you, I have,
Nothing to offer but my love!

~ 94 ~

Being far, is being lost,
Your love is such, it pulls,
Me even closer, to stay in,
Thine arms, I wish forever,
But that pride in your eyes,
It kills me every time,
I wish to express love!

~ 95 ~

She wasn't human to his,
Eyes she was a mannequin,
Made of dirt and clay,
Who had a human lover!
Harsh with his words,
Callous with his touch,
But whenever the world,
Did the same, he fought,
For his mud doll, she was,
Not dead after all,
Alive, she was his wife!

~ 96 ~

The jasmines are not fresh,
Anymore, but my love for you,
Is neither stale, nor has it died,
And if you don't believe,
Then ask those dead buds,
Which I have kept warily,
They will again linger the,
Same elixir of our love,
Into your palm, of days when you,
Lovingly bought me those,
Which I adorned on my coiffure...

~ 97 ~

Why do words become silent?
And the air becomes uncanny,
Why do nights seem long and,
Days clogged, even the clock,
Becomes a punisher, moments,
Are then hard to live by, where,
Does the sleep fly away from eyes?
Whenever thy love has gone far!

~ 98 ~

I know somewhere in the corner,
Of your heart, that love for me,
Hasn't died, but yes! I have to,

Admit, you are a great masquerade
But it was all in your eyes, I read,
And chose being your muse!

~ 99 ~

Whenever the gust flows,
My heart feels thy warmth,
And I think about you in solace,
Knowing that somewhere,
In far the same gust,
Touches you and reminds,
You of me!

~ 100 ~

The autumn's breeze brings the,
Fragrance of the clay from the,
City of Ganges, I am not its part,
Anymore they say, but my,
Soul is made of that same,
Mud, I am made that Goddess!
I shall melt as well one day,
On the day of my immersion

Immersion: Goddess Durga's idol is submerged in a
river on the tenth day according to the Hindu Rituals

About the Author

Monalisa Joshi is a writer and a poetess. As much she loves to write poetry, she also relishes in writing prose and fiction. She is presently working on one of her fiction book and few short stories side by side. She enjoys blogging and is quite active on social media platforms like Facebook and Twitter and she is also an active member of an International poetry group called 'The Awakening poets'. Much of her writings and poetry are showcased in her blogs and can be visited at https://monalisajoshi105.wordpress.com/ and http://monalisa-wwwlisa.blogspot.in/. With a Major in English Literature she feels deeply inspired by Elizabethan poetry and Victorian women poet like Christina Rossetti and thus loves writing ballads and folklores. Her first poetry book is 'Stirring Spoonful of Emotions' from another publisher. Terracotta Dreams is her second poetry book and the title of the book she has chosen to be 'Terracotta Dreams' is because she feels deeply connected to her Indian roots and many of her poems reflects the same earthen essence of her soul. She is also the founder and editor of an online Magazine called "Plethora Blogazine" and finds time for her writing amid the homely chores, her two sons, her husband and a beautiful family life. She balances all her roles with great zest and abundance of love that she fills both in life and her dwelling